I AM PROUD
TO BE A
Catholic!

I AM PROUD TO BE A *Catholic!*

WHAT IS UNIQUE ABOUT BEING A CATHOLIC?

DUANE CROSLAND

authorHOUSE

AuthorHouse™
1663 Liberty Drive
Bloomington, IN 47403
www.authorhouse.com
Phone: 1 (800) 839-8640

© *2016 Duane Crosland. All rights reserved.*

No part of this book may be reproduced, stored in a retrieval system, or transmitted by any means without the written permission of the author.

Published by AuthorHouse 12/02/2016

ISBN: 978-1-5246-4991-3 (sc)
ISBN: 978-1-5246-4989-0 (hc)
ISBN: 978-1-5246-4990-6 (e)

Library of Congress Control Number: 2016918977

Print information available on the last page.

Any people depicted in stock imagery provided by Thinkstock are models, and such images are being used for illustrative purposes only.
Certain stock imagery © Thinkstock.

This book is printed on acid-free paper.

Because of the dynamic nature of the Internet, any web addresses or links contained in this book may have changed since publication and may no longer be valid. The views expressed in this work are solely those of the author and do not necessarily reflect the views of the publisher, and the publisher hereby disclaims any responsibility for them.

Excerpts from the English translation of the Catechism of the Catholic Church for use in the United States of America Copyright © 1994, United States Catholic Conference, Inc. -- Libreria Editrice Vaticana. Used with Permission.

New Revised Standard Version Bible: Anglicised Edition, copyright © 1989, 1995 the Division of Christian Education of the National Council of the Churches of Christ in the United States of America. Used by permission. All rights reserved. Website address – www.nrsvbibles.org.

Dedication

To my parents
Sherman Joseph Crosland
Aurelia Marie Scanlan Crosland
They gave me the gift of Catholicism in baptism

****

To my wife
Kathleen
Kay is my life long Catholic partner

****

To my sons and my daughter-in-laws
Mark, John, Paul, Amber, Heidi, Lucinda
They challenged me to ask why
I am proud to be a Catholic

Acknowledgements

Writing this book has been a five year dream in process. I want to acknowledge a team of friends some of whom simply encouraged my efforts. Many of my supporters are parishioners of St Vincent de Paul Catholic Church, Brooklyn Park, Minnesota (SVDP).

- Crosland, Kay – life time partner and consistent sounding board for my endeavors
- Dufner, Father Thomas – Pastor, Church of the Epiphany, Coon Rapids, Minnesota
- Grisez, Philip – Catechetical Institute, Class of St Francis
- Kiesner, Jack – East coast cousin and retired Editor of the Kiplinger Newsletter
- Kiesner, LaDonna – East coast cousin
- Krynski, Gloria – SVDP parishioner and friend
- Kuzma, Jennifer – SVDP parishioner and friend
- Moorman, Nancy – SVDP parishioner, friend and Catechetical Institute, Class of St Francis
- Newstrom, Betty – West coast cousin and retired Secretary for Evangelization, Spokane WA
- Niemczyk, Peggy – Catechetical Institute, Class of St Francis
- Peick, Rob – cousin, English professor and ruthless editor of my material
- Pikovsky, Cindy – SVDP parishioner, friend and Catechetical Institute, Class of St Francis
- Pratt, Chuck – Director of Faith Formation, SVDP
- Wahlquist, Kelly – Catechetical Institute, Catholic author and speaker

- Table of Contents -

Introduction

Opening Comments.. 3
I was born and baptized a Catholic 4
I was raised a Catholic... 5
I lived a life of a Catholic.. 6
Being a Catholic in the 21st Century 8
The Book 11

I am Proud to be a Catholic

Introduction to Jesus Christ..................................... 15
Catholic Church... 19
The Pope.. 21
The Catholic Mass 23
The Eucharist... 31
The Consecration 35
Altar of a Catholic Church 37
Seven Sacraments 40
Sacrament of Reconciliation 43
Sign of the Cross 46
Catechism of the Catholic Church 48
God's Covenants with Man...................................... 51
Precepts of the Church 54
Perpetual Adoration... 56
Catholic Social Teaching... 58
Stations of the Cross 61

Mary, the Mother of God 63
Rosary 66
Catholic Priest 70
The Communion of Saints 74
The Church Triumphant 75
The Beatitudes 79
Faith – A Belief in God 81
Scandals of the Catholic Church 85
The Catholic Church in the World Today 88

Closing Comments

On a Personal Note 95

Appendix

Index of Religions & Date of Origination 101
Fifteen Promises of Mary 103
Local and National Catholic Resources 105
Common Catholic Prayers 106

Introduction

Opening Comments

If you bought this book looking for controversy or evidence of a major religious re-birth by the author, you bought the wrong book. Ask for your money back.

The intention of this book is simply to articulate why I am proud to be a Catholic. If you are a practicing Catholic, you have heard most of the detail that is presented in this book but it may not have been in a concise format that you could share with your loved ones.

Hopefully, this book can be used by –

- A teacher who will share these thoughts with his/her students on a weekly basis.
- A parent who will read from this book to his/her children as to why they, the parents, are proud to be a Catholic.
- A grandparent who will give this book as a gift to a grandchild for First Communion or Confirmation.
- A friend, sponsor, teacher who will give this book as a gift to a Rite of Christian Initiation of Adults (RCIA) candidate when received into the Catholic Church.
- Yourself to confirm or clarify the teachings of the Catholic faith.

I have purposely kept this book simple so that it can be enjoyed by all, including children and young adults.

I was born and baptized a Catholic

I was born Duane Sherman Crosland to Sherman Joseph Crosland and Aurelia Marie Scanlan Crosland. My mother and dad were devout practicing Catholics.

My grandparents on both my mother's and dad's family were practicing Catholics.

I was baptized at Saint Luke's Catholic Church, Saint Paul, Minnesota. My godparents were my mother's twin sister, Elizabeth (Aunt Betty) Scanlan Peick, and her husband, Robert (Uncle Bob) Peick.

I was raised a Catholic

I have 16 years of Catholic education, having graduated from Saint Mark's Grade School, Cretin High School and the College of Saint Thomas (1965), all located in Saint Paul, Minnesota.

For two years in grade school, my sister and I lived too far from the Catholic grade school to walk. My parents sent us by taxi every day so that we might attend a Catholic school. My parents had an exceptionally strong commitment to their religious beliefs.

My dad died when I was 10 years old. My generous grandparents shared a large, comfortable home with my mother, two sisters and me. In addition, our family depended heavily on my godparents. Every Sunday my aunt and uncle would come to pick us up for church. We squeezed three adults and eight children into a two door sedan to get to Saint Mark's church. Needless to say, we did not wear seat belts.

Too many times to count, I walked the two and a half miles roundtrip by myself for other church activities including the Sacrament of Reconciliation on Saturday afternoons.

We always attended Christmas Midnight Mass and the Holy Thursday, Good Friday, Holy Saturday and Easter celebrations as a family.

I lived a life of a Catholic

While in the Air Force and on my personal travels I attended Catholic churches in Hong Kong, Japan, Taiwan, India, and Thailand. Often, I could not understand the words being spoken, but I was still able to follow the Mass. Stationed in Taiwan for three years I attended Sunday mass on the base; in addition, I was an officer in the *Holy Name of Jesus Society*, lector for Sunday Mass, the editor for the monthly church newsletter and a member of the church choir.

Returning from military service at the age of 26, I attended the Cathedral of Saint Paul for Sunday Mass. I often sat in this very large building and was awed by its majesty and beauty. If you closed your eyes, it was easy to understand the devotion to the Catholic Church that our ancestors had. The Cathedral, built 100 years ago, mostly from donations by ordinary working people, is a witness to their solid faith.

Looking for a social life, I joined the Minneapolis Dominic Club, a group for Catholic singles 21 and over.

I had a number of criteria in looking for my life time partner. My primary criterion was that she and her family had to be practicing Catholics.

Unbeknownst to Kay and me, I found my life time partner at the first Dominic Club event I attended in April 1970.

In addition to being a practicing Catholic, Kay had an exceptional mother, father, and extended family.

Our first date was in August 1970. Kay and I were married on Saturday, July 24, 1971, at the beautiful Saint Anne's Catholic Church in north Minneapolis. We had four priests in attendance – the pastor,

I Am Proud to Be a Catholic!

the prior pastor, a friend from Chicago, and the chaplain from North Memorial Hospital, where Kay worked as a registered nurse (RN). With four priests in attendance, it would be hard to back out of this marriage!

Kay and I were blessed with three healthy boys. Mark and John were baptized at the Church of Saint Raphael in Crystal Minnesota. Paul was baptized at Saint Joseph the Worker in Maple Grove, Minnesota.

The front pew on the left side of the Saint Joseph the Worker church belonged to the Croslands. We sat in the front pew so that our boys could see what was happening on the altar. Kay and I were active at our church – the religious education program, social justice board, usher, summer festival, men's club, etc.

We missed Sunday Mass only once as a family. It was in the Teton Mountains. We carefully made plans to attend a local church as a part of our schedule, only to find that the Mass had been cancelled due to a celebration in Jackson Hole, Wyoming. We attended a weekday Mass once we returned home.

All three sons made the rank of Eagle Scout and were recognized by the scouts and the Catholic Church for their accomplishments.

During 2001 and 2002 John and Paul were married with our friend, the parish deacon, in attendance; John was married in Bend, Oregon, and Paul at our parish church, Saint Joseph the Worker in Maple Grove, Minnesota.

Being a Catholic in the 21st Century

Then all three sons stopped going to Sunday Mass. Maybe they knew something that I did not. The result was an enormous amount of soul searching by Kay and me. Where did we go wrong? What did we fail to do? Why? Why? Why?

At the same time the sexual scandals within the Catholic Church were making headlines in the daily newspaper.

I started to question my belief in the Catholic Church; the doubting Thomas within me began to gain ground.

Fortunately, the powers of good were pulling me in the opposite direction, thanks to God's gift of faith which He so generously shared with me.

In retrospect I was an active Catholic for sixty years in what I would call "coast mode." For sixty years, my relationship with God ran on automatic pilot. There simply was no need to question my faith. When my sons stopped going to church, I began to ask myself questions –

- Why am I a Catholic?
- What do I believe as a Catholic?
- Should I be proud to be a Catholic?

I could not articulate my beliefs. I was confused and frustrated. I realized that I was unable to answer questions my sons and daughters-in-law brought to me.

Then in the spring of 2005 I retired, and my life, as a Catholic, began to come into focus.

I Am Proud to Be a Catholic!

- I set for myself three goals for my life as a retiree: do good for others, build a stronger relationship with my God and have fun!
- I signed up for a weekly visit to the Saint Louis Chapel of Perpetual Adoration at Saint Vincent de Paul Catholic Church, Brooklyn Park, Minnesota. An hour a week in the physical presence of Jesus Christ is an awesome experience!
- In the chapel, I found a book written by Jeff Cavins titled *"I'm Not Being Fed."* The focus of the book is the Eucharist. I started reading the book during Perpetual Adoration and brought it home to finish that night. I could not wait a week to the read the remaining pages. I read the book once and then twice and then three times. The book gave me the basis as to why I am a Catholic and why "I am proud to be a Catholic." It is said that if you give God a chance to talk to you, He will. This book was God's way of talking to me in the silence of the Saint Louis Chapel as I searched for answers.
- I also had a short conversation with our Parochial Vicar, Father Peter Williams. He told me that all of my distractions, including the sex scandals within the Church, were the work of the devil and that I should keep my focus on the Eucharist. These few words were another insight that gave me the basis as to why I am a Catholic and why I am proud to be a Catholic.
- At the age of 62, I signed up to teach fourth grade religious education on Wednesday afternoons. At 72, I may be the oldest person in the faith formation program at our church. I found the fourth grade curriculum rich with Catholic beliefs:

  – Beatitudes
  – Ten Commandments
  – Corporal and Spiritual Works of Mercy
  – Mass
  – Eucharist
  – Gifts and Fruits of the Holy Spirit
  – Cardinal and Theological Virtues
  – Church Precepts
  – And, much, much more.

Little did my students know that I was getting more out of my classes than they were. In teaching my fourth grade religious education classes, I asked my students why they were a Catholic. I asked them what made them proud to be Catholic. I faced total silence. Most of my students were operating in the same vacuum that I was. I began the practice of telling my students that I was proud to be a Catholic; and I would tell them why I was proud to be a Catholic. Details of what I shared with my students are the content of this book.

- As a part of my religious education class, I wrote weekly letters that I sent home to the parents telling them what we covered in class. Then I would add a paragraph about some of the golden treasures of the Catholic faith. I would begin this section of the letter with "On a personal note - I am proud to be a Catholic." After writing letters to the parents for a couple of years, I decided it was time to put my writings into a book.

The Book

The book was to be called

I Am Proud to be a CATHOLIC.

All the beliefs listed in this book are unique to being a Catholic. All the beliefs listed in this book reveal the beauty of the Catholic Church.

Every one of us is on a faith journey – each journey is unique.

After 60 years of coasting as a Catholic and 12 years of soul searching, I can now tell you why I am a Catholic. I finally have some direction to my faith journey.

Each chapter in this book is an explanation of why I am a Catholic and why I love being a Catholic.

Interesting side stories –

- In the fall of 2014 Bishop Andrew Cozzens from the Archdiocese of Saint Paul / Minneapolis talked at our parish one Sunday evening. He started by asking a gentleman in the first pew why he was a Catholic. His response was "I did not have much choice in the decision." A second gentleman responded with "I was baptized a Catholic" and then shrugged his shoulders.
- As I wrote this book, I asked a close friend of mine why he was a Catholic. His response was "I was baptized a Catholic." He could not provide any additional justification as to why he was a Catholic except that he was comfortable with the religion he grew up with.

None of the three gentlemen could say why they were a Catholic. Their responses further justify the need for a book such as this. Every Catholic should be able to say "I am proud to be a Catholic because …………"

This book reveals no new dogmas; it is not intended to create religious controversy; it does not have an imprimatur from the local bishop. This book is written to share with everyone the unique beliefs of the Catholic Church in a very simple format from my perspective.

Clarification - the twelve primary rites of the Catholic Church are:

- Roman
- Byzantine
- Syrian
- Maronite
- Chaldean
- Malankar
- Armenian
- Coptic
- Ethiopian
- Malabar
- Ambrosian
- Mozarabic.

I and most readers of this book, I surmise, belong to the Roman Rite. All twelve rites are in union with the Papacy of Rome and therefore all the rites listed above share the same beliefs in Jesus and the church. We all celebrate the seven sources of grace, the Sacraments, and we all observe the Ten Commandments. We have different languages and customs but we are all united in the one, holy, catholic and apostolic Catholic Church.

Let us begin –

I AM PROUD
TO BE A
Catholic!

Introduction to Jesus Christ

If you are not of the Catholic faith and are reading this book, please take time to tell me about the person who founded your church – Martin Luther, King Henry the VIII, John Calvin, Joseph Smith, John and Charles Wesley, John Smyth, Charles Taze Russell, Mohammed or maybe a vibrant homilist – a twenty-first century man or woman from your community – possibly from a large suburban mega church.

~~~~~~~~~~**********~~~~~~~~~~

Then, I would like to introduce you to the God/Man, Jesus Christ, who gave us the Catholic Church. Let me start with selected lines of the Apostles' Creed –

I believe in God, the Father almighty,
creator of Heaven and earth,
**and in Jesus Christ,
his only Son, Our Lord,
who was conceived by the Holy Spirit,
born of the Virgin Mary,
suffered under Pontius Pilate,
was crucified, died, and was buried;
he descended into hell;
on the third day he rose again from the dead;
he ascended into heaven and
is seated at the right hand of God
the Father almighty;
from there he will come again
to judge the living and the dead.**

While on earth, during his three years of public life, the source and Founder of the Catholic Church, Jesus Christ –

- Turned water into wine at the marriage feast of Cana (John 2)
- Gave sight to the blind (John 9)
- Raised the dead (John 11)
- Fed five thousand men with five loaves and two fishes (John 6)
- Calmed a storm (Luke 8)
- Forgave men of their sins (Matthew 9)
- Cured the ten men of leprosy (Luke 17)
- Healed the centurion's servant (Matthew 8)
- Cast out demons (Matthew 9 & 17)
- Cured a deaf man (Mark 7)
- Walked on water (Mark 6)
- Appeared with Moses and Elijah in the Transfiguration (Mark 9)

In addition to the miracles listed above, Jesus Christ -

- Gave us the Great Commandment to love God and your neighbor (Matthew 22)
- Taught us how to pray - giving us the Lord's Prayer (Matthew 6)
- Gave us the Sermon on the Mount / the Beatitudes (Matthew 5)
- Modeled a lesson of service and humility washing the feet of the apostles (John 13)
- Instituted the Sacrament of the Eucharist at the Last Supper (Matthew 26, Mark 14, Luke 22)

And twice, God the Father and God the Holy Spirit gave witness that Jesus Christ was truly the Son of God sent to redeem man from his sins-

> **And when Jesus had been baptized, just as he came from the water, suddenly the heavens were opened to him and he saw the Spirit of God descending like a dove and alighting on him. And a voice from**

I Am Proud to Be a Catholic!

heaven said, "This is my Son, the Beloved, with whom I am well pleased. (Matthew 3:16-17, NRSV)

And he was transfigured before them, and his face shone like the sun, and his clothes became dazzling white. Suddenly there appeared to them Moses and Elijah, talking with him. While he was still speaking, suddenly a bright cloud overshadowed them, and from a cloud a voice said, "This is my Son, the Beloved; with him I am well pleased; listen to him!" (Matthew 3:2-3 & 3:5, NRSV)

It is estimated that there are over 33,000 Christian variations/ denominations founded by thousands of "human beings" over the past 500 years since the Reformation – all of them trying to improve on what Jesus Christ, Himself, gave to us.

All non-Catholic Christian churches (ecclesial communities) are variations about Jesus Christ. Only the Catholic Church is Jesus Christ. Only the Catholic Church can claim that their Founder and Foundation still lives. Need I say more?

See the index in the back of the book for a list of the world's most prominent religious founders.

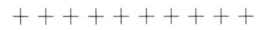

+ + + + + + + + + +

Personal opportunities / challenges -

+ *Given that there are 33,000 Christian denominations in the world today read John 17:20-21 where Jesus asks His Father that we all may be one. Read, meditate, pray, contemplate.*
+ *Read "The Catholic Church Through the Ages" by John Vidmar, OP to understand the challenges, failures and triumphs of the Catholic Church over the past 2000 years. Learn and understand*

the origin of the schisms of the one Church that Jesus Christ gave to us.

+ *Come to a Catholic Mass or to any Catholic church that has Perpetual Adoration and meet the founder / foundation of the Catholic Church in person! He is waiting for you!*
+ *Share with your child, your grandchild, your students and your friends the excitement about the Man who gave us the Catholic Church. Remind them that Jesus Christ gave us one Church and it is the Catholic Church.*

Catholic Church

Jesus Christ founded one church, and it is the Catholic Church!

> ***And I tell you, you are Peter and on this rock I will build my church and the gates of Hades will not prevail against it.*** (Matthew 16:18, NRSV)

As Jesus Christ had promised, 2000 years later the church that He founded grows in beauty and strength.

Despite human frailties, heresies, scandals, false prophets, schisms, martyrdoms and outright challenges to its very existence throughout the centuries, the Church continues to be the sole source of the full range of graces promised to us by Jesus Christ.

The core doctrines, beliefs, traditions and practices of the church have remained true to the teachings of Jesus Christ.

The Church founded by Jesus Christ is <u>one</u>, <u>holy</u>, <u>catholic</u>, and <u>apostolic</u>.

The Church is <u>one</u> because her source, founder and spirit are one in the Holy Trinity of God the Father, Son and Holy Spirit.

The Church is <u>holy</u> because Jesus Christ, the Son of God, who with the Father and the Spirit is hailed as "alone holy."

The Church is <u>catholic</u> or universal because she proclaims the fullness of the faith and is sent out to all peoples. The Church is inclusive of all people.

The Church is <u>apostolic</u> because Christ assigned its leadership on earth to Peter, specifically, and the apostles, collectively, who are present in their successors, the current Pope and the college of bishops.

Duane Crosland

+ + + + + + + + + +

Personal opportunities / challenges -

- + One – although one in God, the church consists of a wide range of diversity across the world. This can be witnessed as one travels around the world. If the opportunity presents itself, attend a local Catholic Church in another part of the world to understand both the diversity and oneness of the organization.
- + Holy – reminder the Church is Holy; its members are not! We are all sinners attempting to be holy.
- + Catholic - look at a map of the world. Understand the size of the Catholic Church when you say it is universal. The Catholic Church extends its reach from Siberia in northern Russia to the tip of the Antarctica. Every square inch of the world reports to Rome through a diocese.
- + Apostolic – when at Mass next Sunday, realize the powers exercised by the priests have been handed down from the apostles through the bishops to all Catholic priests over the past 2,000 years. The apostolic link within the Catholic Church has never been broken.
- + Read the Catechism of the Catholic Church (CCC) paragraphs 811 through 870 for further definition of the four marks of the Catholic Church.

The Pope

Pope Francis is a direct successor to our first pope, St Peter; he is the 266th pope to follow in the footsteps of Peter.

The tomb of St Peter, the man who walked with Jesus, talked with Jesus, ate with Jesus on a daily basis, the man who denied Jesus three times, the man who died for his church 2000 years ago, can be found at the foundation of the altar of the Basilica of St Peter's in Rome.

In Matthew 16, Jesus names Peter as the first leader of His church giving him the keys to the kingdom of heaven -

> *I will give you the <u>keys of the kingdom of heaven</u>, and whatever you bind on earth will be bound in heaven, and whatever you loose on earth will be loosed in heaven.* (Matthew 16:19, NRSV)

These are truly powerful words! The Apostolic Powers, the "keys" given by Jesus to Simon Peter to govern His people are now held by Pope Francis, the leader of the Catholic Church.

These keys are shared by the pope with bishops, priests and deacons across the world.

The keys of the Kingdom of Heaven -

- Gives the gift of infallibility to the Catholic Church in her objective definitive teaching regarding faith and morals.
- Empowers a priest to change bread and wine into the body and blood of Christ during the Liturgy of the Eucharist.
- Empowers a priest to forgive sin in the Sacrament of Reconciliation and the Sacrament of the Sick.

- Empowers a bishop to ordain men to the priesthood and deaconship.
- Empowers a bishop to confirm and strengthen a member of the Church with the Holy Spirit.
- Empowers the pope to recognize men and woman who led an exemplary and holy life canonizing them as saints.

The keys of the Kingdom of Heaven reside specifically with the ministry of Peter and the apostles and their successors.

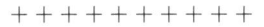

++++++++++

Personal opportunities / challenges -

+ *Read "John Paul II – A Personal Portrait of the Pope and the Man" by Ray Flynn, former United States Ambassador to the Vatican. The book documents the life of a pope of the Catholic Church as witnessed by Ray Flynn – John Paul II, a current day pope who is now a saint.*
+ *On the internet access a painting by Pietro Perugino showing Peter accepting the keys (symbol of authority) of the Catholic Church from Jesus Christ.*
+ *Pray daily for the safety of our pope given the international threats against his life.*

The Catholic Mass

The Catholic Mass is a beautiful prayer! It is the celebration of the Word of God and the celebration of the Holy Eucharist – the Liturgy of the Word and the Liturgy of the Eucharist.

If you look at the Mass as simply a weekly obligation, it can be a long hour. Take the time to understand the various parts of the Mass. Each part of the Mass is unique and adds to the beauty of the overall celebration. The hymns, prayers, readings, the Consecration can all be traced to either the Old or New Testament and 2,000 years of Catholic tradition.

The Mass explores the vast depths of our understanding of God. The Mass is a celebration of God the Father, God the Son and God the Holy Spirit.

This is the longest chapter of the book. Bear with me on this subject. There is so much to cover.

The Mass originated with the Last Supper when Jesus broke the bread and blessed the wine. Then after His resurrection Jesus confirmed His will that the Last Supper be celebrated among His followers. Jesus, Himself, celebrated the Mass during the Walk to Emmaus with two of his disciples as recorded by Saint Luke.

The Liturgy of the Word –

> **Then beginning with Moses and all the prophets, he interpreted to them the things about Himself in all the scriptures.** (Luke 24:27, NRSV)

Duane Crosland

The Liturgy of the Eucharist –

When He was at the table with them, He took bread, blessed and broke it, and gave it to them. Then their eyes were opened, and they recognized Him; and He vanished from sight. (Luke 24:30-31, NRSV)

In taking a class at the Archbishop Harry J. Flynn Catechetical Institute through the Saint Paul Seminary, Saint Paul, Minnesota, I learned of writings from Saint Justin Martyr, dated 155 A.D., where he writes a summary of the Mass for pagan emperor Antoninus Pius (138-161).

On the next page is a comparison of today's Mass to the writings of Saint Justin Martyr (CCC 1345). Today's Mass is the same Mass celebrated 2000 years ago!

I Am Proud to Be a Catholic!

2014 A.D.		The Mass documented by St Justin Martyr in the Year 155 A.D.
The Mass	Introductory Rite	On the day we call the day of the sun, all who dwell in the city or country gather in the same place.
	Liturgy of the Word	The memoirs of the apostles and the writings of the prophets are read, as much as time permits. When the reader has finished, he who presides over those gathered admonishes and challenges them to imitate these beautiful things. Then we all rise together and offer prayers for ourselves … for others, wherever they may be, so that we may be found righteous by our life and actions, faithful to the commandments, so as to obtain eternal salvation. When the prayers are concluded we exchange the kiss.
	Liturgy of the Eucharist	Then someone brings bread and a cup of water and wine mixed together to him who presides over the brethren. He takes them and offers praise and glory to the Father of the universe, through the name of the Son and of the Holy Spirit and for a considerable time he gives thanks that we have been judged worthy of these gifts. When he has concluded the prayers and thanksgivings, all present give voice to an acclamation by saying: 'Amen.' When he who presides has given thanks and the people have responded, those whom we call deacons give to those present the "eucharisted" bread, wine and water …
	Concluding Rite	… and take them to those who are absent.

As documented in the summary above, the Mass consists of four parts –

- <u>Introductory Rite</u>

    – We sing an opening hymn supporting the theme of the Sunday gospel.
    – The celebrant makes welcoming comments.
    – The celebrant leads us in an opening prayer asking for God's blessing upon our celebration.
    – We ask for God's forgiveness for our failings of the past week – mea culpa!
    – We praise God for all of his amazing attributes in the <u>Gloria</u>. We proclaim God's power, glory and magnificence throughout this prayer - the prayer inspired by the angels at the birth of Christ in Bethlehem

    Gloria to God in the highest heaven, and on earth peace among those whom He favors!
    (Luke 2:14, NRSV)

- <u>Liturgy of the Word</u>

    – We listen to the first reading taken from either the Old or New Testament of the Bible depending on the season of the Church.
    – We respond with a Psalm from the Old Testament. The Psalms, consisting of 150 poems, hymns and prayers, covers the full range of Israel's religious faith and has become a treasured book of worship by Christians.
    – We listen to the second reading taken from the New Testament. These readings are letters from one of the early leaders of the church.
    – We listen to the Gospel from one of the four evangelists – Matthew, Mark, Luke and John. The first three Gospels are cycled over a three year period. John is used for special occasions.

- We listen to the homily in support of the scripture readings. The homily makes the Sunday readings relevant to today's challenges and opportunities.
- We clearly state our beliefs as a Catholic with the Creed. We confirm our belief in God the Father, Son and Holy Spirit and all that the Catholic Church teaches – "I believe in…."
- We pray the General Intercessions asking for graces from God for specific needs – our religious and national leaders, the sick of the parish, peace in the world, special intentions and finally our personal intentions.

- Liturgy of the Eucharist

  - Preparation of the altar and our gifts of bread and wine, washing of the celebrant's hands.
  - Eucharistic Prayer -

    - Preface Prayer over the gifts asking God to accept them.
    - Preface Acclamation – Holy, holy, holy – again we honor God's glory, a prayer of praise!
    - **The Consecration / the celebration of the Last Supper – our gifts of bread and wine become the Body and Blood of Christ through the intercession of the Holy Spirit.** Christ's promise to be with us until the end of time becomes a reality!
    - Memorial Acclamation – we confirm our belief in the death and the resurrection of Jesus Christ.
    - We then petition that our prayers join with those of the Virgin Mary and the saints for the wellbeing of our pope, bishops, priests and all of God's people living and dead.
    - Depending on the church season or the designated celebration of the day, additional prayers may be added to the Eucharistic Prayer.

- Doxology - "Through Him, with Him and in Him, in the unity of the Holy Spirit, all glory and honor is yours, almighty Father, forever and ever."

  – The Lord's Prayer given to us by Jesus Christ, Himself, to honor God the Father.
  – Rite of Peace / the kiss of peace.
  – Breaking of the Bread just as Jesus did at the Last Supper – Lord, have mercy on us; grant us peace.
  – Communion or the distribution of the Eucharistic Body and Blood. **The recipient now holds Jesus Christ, the Son of God, in the palm of his hand!**
  – Prayer after Communion.

- <u>Concluding Rite</u>

  – Closing prayer which can be a Simple Blessing, Solemn Blessing, prayer over the people or Pontifical Blessing.
  – Dismissal or the final blessing – "Go in peace to love and serve the Lord".
  – Closing hymn supporting the theme of the Sunday gospel.

The Mass is the framework for the sacraments of the Eucharist, Confirmation and Holy Orders and on request the sacraments of Baptism and Matrimony. The Mass is also the core celebration of a Catholic funeral.

Out of respect for the House of God, the reception of the Eucharist, the priest and your fellow parishioners, a person should arrive early and leave only after the priest has left the sanctuary. At the end of Mass spend time in the gathering area of the church to exchange words of support and to build on the fellowship celebrated during the Mass.

To enrich your participation in the Mass, volunteer to become a server, lector, greeter, usher, extraordinary minister of the Eucharist, or member of the choir.

I Am Proud to Be a Catholic!

Every Catholic Church, every Catholic Mass has its own unique feel, tempo, music, practices, architecture, arrangements and level of personal involvement. Find a Catholic Church that meets your needs and then participate fully. A Catholic Church located in downtown St Paul, Minnesota celebrates Mass in 30 minutes. A Catholic Mass in the Caribbean is celebrated in 90 minutes plus. The Mass is the same whether it is 30 minutes or 90 minutes.

Regardless of the unique feel, the Catholic Mass is universal. The Catholic Mass has been, is and will be consistent across all generations and across all people.

The Mass that we celebrate daily at my church, St Vincent de Paul, located in Brooklyn Park, Minnesota is the same Mass that the early Christians celebrated – the Liturgy of the Word and the Liturgy of the Eucharist. The Mass that we celebrate daily at St Vincent de Paul is the same Mass celebrated in New Delhi, Tokyo, Waikiki, San Diego, New York, Paris, and the Saint Peter's Basilica located in Rome.

Twenty four hours a day, seven days a week somewhere in the world the bread and wine are consecrated to become the Body and Blood of Christ.

The Catholic Church requires weekly attendance at Mass on Sundays and Holy Days of Obligation. The Church clearly understands the importance of the Mass and the gift of the Eucharist and thus the requirement. Once a Catholic aligns with the Church on the importance of the Mass, attendance is no longer a requirement but Mass is anticipated as a weekly gift from Jesus Christ, a participation in the sacrifice on Calvary, a sharing of the gift from the Last Supper.

No matter where you travel, "home" can always be found at a Catholic Mass.

Duane Crosland

+ + + + + + + + + +

Personal opportunities / challenges –

+ On Sunday morning leave your watch at home! Understand that the Mass is not one continuous blur. Every prayer and/or action is <u>uniquely selected</u> to celebrate the Liturgy of the Word and Liturgy of the Eucharist. Examples – when we sing the Kyrie eleison (Lord, have mercy) remind yourself that we are asking God's forgiveness for our transgressions of the past week; when you stand for the Gospel, remind yourself that Jesus is sharing the mind of His Father with us; when the Host is raised during the Consecration, remind yourself that the words of the Last Supper changes the bread into the body of Christ. Get serious about learning background details of the Mass. Mass will no longer be a "time" thing.
+ Get to Mass early; participate; do not leave Mass early. The priest should be the last person coming into church and the first person to leave the church.
+ To more deeply understand the Mass, read "The Mass" by Edward Sri. The book provides the reader with a thorough background of the Mass with a detailed biblical walk through of all liturgical prayers and actions.
+ Daily Mass is highly recommended. If you are not a morning person or your schedule does not allow for a morning Mass, check your neighboring churches for a mid-day or an evening Mass.
+ When attending Mass wear clothes that are appropriate for the occasion. Would you were a pair of worn jeans if you were invited to the White House to meet the president? Would you wear a pair of shorts with flip-flops if the Queen of England had invited you to tea some afternoon? If you were invited to a reception at the Louvre by the President of France, would you wear beach clothes? If you truly believed that you were going to spend an hour with Jesus at Mass, what would you wear?

The Eucharist

In the Old Testament (Exodus 16:12), God feeds His people manna in the desert. In the New Testament Jesus feeds five thousand with five loaves and two fish (Matthew 14:13-21, Mark 6:30-44, Luke 9:10-17 and John 6:1-14). Both events are a foretelling of the bread of life as promised by Jesus and recorded by John -

> *So Jesus said to them, "Very truly, I tell you, unless you eat the flesh of the Son of Man and drink his blood, you have no life in you. Those who eat my flesh and drink my blood have eternal life, and I will raise them up on the last day; for my flesh is true food and my blood is true drink. Those who eat my flesh and drink my blood abide in me and I in them. Just as the living Father sent me, I live because of the Father, so whoever eats me will live because of me. This is the bread that came down from heaven, not like that which your ancestors ate, and they died. But the one who eats this bread will live forever."* (John 6: 53-58, NRSV)

As we continue to read John, Jesus clarifies and reinforces His statement for the nonbelievers.

> *Because of this many of his disciples turned back and no longer went with him.* (John 6:66, NRSV)

Then on the night before His death, at the Last Supper, in the upper room, Jesus gave us the gift of His Body and Blood as He promised His followers in the gospel of John.

> **While they were eating, He took a loaf of bread, and after blessing it He broke it, gave it to them,**

> and said, "Take; this is My Body." Then He took a cup, and after giving thanks He gave it to them, and all drank from it. He said to them, "This is My Blood of the covenant, which is poured out for many." (Mark 14:22-24, NRSV)

At risk of being repetitive - after His resurrection in the Walk to Emmaus with two of his disciples, Jesus confirmed His gift to us.

> **When He was at the table with them, he took bread, blessed and broke it, and gave it to them.** (Luke 24:30, NRSV)

Every time we attend Mass we have the opportunity to have a physical relationship with Jesus Christ.

Every time we attend Mass, we have the opportunity to receive the Holy Eucharist, Jesus' precious body and blood, soul and divinity.

In the palm of our hands we hold the body of Jesus Christ, we hold the Eucharist; we hold the God who created the universe, the God who made you and me. In the chalice, we hold the blood of Jesus Christ, we hold the Eucharist; we hold the God who created the universe, the God who made you and me.

> *My Lord and my God!* (John 20:28, NRSV)

The Eucharist is a living gift from Jesus Christ twenty four hours a day, seven days a week. This is the food that nourishes and refreshes our souls and our bodies.

> *I am the bread of life.* (John 6:48, NRSV)

The Eucharist is the fulfillment of the promise made by Jesus Christ to his apostles that He will be with His Church until the end of the time.

The Eucharist is the source and summit of the Christian life. (CCC 1324)

The reception of the Eucharist should truly be a moment of wonder and awe for every Catholic! The Eucharist is what makes a person a Catholic. The Eucharist clearly defines and confirms our belief in the teachings of Jesus Christ!

Many of Jesus' followers left him when He told them that He would give them His Body to eat and His Blood to drink. How could bread and wine turn into the Body and Blood of Christ? With God anything is possible.

- Jesus told Lazarus to rise from the dead. Lazarus rose from the dead. How? God willed it!
- Jesus turned water into wine at the wedding feast of Cana. How? God willed it!
- Jesus told the wind to stop and the sea to go calm. The wind stopped and the sea went calm. How? God willed it!
- Jesus told the lame to walk, the sick to take up their beds, the blind to see. How? God willed it!
- Jesus lay in the tomb for three days but rose triumphantly from the dead. How? God willed it!
- Jesus turned bread and wine into His Body and Blood at the Last Supper. How? God willed it!
- A Catholic priest turns our gifts of bread and wine into the Body and Blood of Christ at the Consecration of the Mass. How? God wills it.

Quoting Saint Cyril of Jerusalem –

Since Christ Himself has said, "This is My Body" who shall dare to doubt that It is His Body?

Duane Crosland

+ + + + + + + + + +

Personal opportunities / challenges -

+ On receiving the Body of Christ in the palm of your hand momentarily hold and gaze at the Body of Jesus Christ, the Word Incarnate, that died and rose from the dead for you! Share your most intimate thoughts, praise and requests with Jesus Christ at this time.
+ Jeff Cavins has written a beautiful book, "I'M NOT BEING FED!" on the Eucharist with a subtitle of "Discovering the Food that Satisfies the Soul". I encourage you to read his book.
+ Read and meditate on John 6:22-71 where Jesus very clearly foretells His gift of the Eucharist and then witness the reaction of His followers. "Because of this many of His disciples turned back and no longer went about with Him" (John 6:66, NRSV). What do you believe? Would you have left Jesus when He promised you His Body to eat and His Blood to drink? Personally, I might have.
+ The church across town may be led by an awe inspiring homilist; it may have music that is guaranteed to lift the soul week after week; it may have the latest in video and audio technology; it may have soaring and inspirational architect; it may have a committee at the front door every Sunday to welcome you. But only in a Catholic Church can you meet Jesus in a physical form through the Eucharist. Come and receive His Body and Blood, Soul and Divinity – the gift that Jesus, Himself, gave to all of us at the Last Supper. What and where are your priorities?

The Consecration

The Consecration is the fulfillment of the promise of the Eucharist.

The Eucharistic prayer is the most important prayer in the Catholic Church. The prayer found in the Liturgy of the Eucharist begins with the Preface Prayer and ends with the Doxology. These prayers form the framework to the Consecration.

The Consecration of the Catholic Mass is a direct participation in the same meal that Jesus shared with his twelve apostles 2000 years ago at the Last Supper.

Stop and think of the significance of these statements.

> ***Then he took a loaf of bread, and when he had given thanks, he broke it and gave it to them, saying "This is my body, which is given for you. Do this in remembrance of me."*** *(*Luke 22:19, NRSV)

> ***And he did the same with the cup after supper, saying "This cup that is poured out for you is the new covenant in my blood."*** *(*Luke 22: 20, NRSV)

Our gifts of bread and wine become, by the powers given to a priest at the time of his ordination, the Body and Blood of Jesus Christ.

This is the moment in time when heaven and earth touch.

Duane Crosland

++++++++++

Personal opportunities / challenges -

+ *Let your imagination run wide - we firmly believe that at the moment of the Consecration - God the Father, through intercession of the Holy Spirit, sends His Son, Jesus, to be Body, Blood, Soul and Divinity present within our midst. And God goes nowhere without a host of heavenly angels. Stand in awe at the spiritual celebration within the walls of our church at the time of the Consecration.*
+ *The priest elevates the Body of Christ and then genuflects. The priest then elevates the chalice containing the Blood of Christ and then genuflects. We have met our King!*
+ *If the Most Valuable Player (MVP) from this year's NFL Champion football team or the winning actress from last night's Oscar presentations had just entered the room where would our attention be?*
+ *Volunteer to become an Extraordinary Eucharist Minister. Participate in the distribution of the gift from heaven.*

Altar of a Catholic Church

The altar table of a Catholic Church is the center and core of a Catholic worship space; it is the focal point of the Catholic Mass.

At the beginning of Mass the book of the four gospels is placed at the center of the altar table until the gospel is read during the Liturgy of the Word. For the Liturgy of the Eucharist, the bread and wine are prepared and then changed into the Body and Blood of Christ on the altar table.

The altar serves as the "Last Supper" table from which the Eucharist is shared with those in communion with the Catholic Church.

The concept of an altar goes back to the book of Genesis when Abraham was told to build an altar to offer his son as a sacrifice to God. Throughout the Old Testament, the Jewish people offered various produce and animals to God as a sacrifice on the temple altar. In the New Testament the table at the Last Supper became the altar of the new covenant.

To a Catholic, the altar is a sacred space. The priest kisses the altar at the beginning of Mass and at the end of Mass to show his respect. Catholics on entering a church or leaving a church either bow to the altar or genuflect depending on the location of the Tabernacle to show their understanding of the sacredness of the altar and surrounding space.

In 2010, Kay and I travelled to Orlando, Florida for our quick break from a Minnesota winter. We heard that a new church had opened in Celebration, a subdivision of Disney World, and we decided to attend the Saturday evening Mass. We arrived our normal 15 minutes early only to find the parking lot full and the church filled to capacity. We came upon the dedication of the Corpus Christi Catholic Church! Our one hour service became a two hour experience.

The dedication became a once in a life time experience – truly a spiritual blessing. Below are quotes from the program given to us as we entered the church. I quote freely from the program since the wording is beautiful in its simplicity and could not be explained better if it were rephrased.

> **Anointing of the Altar** - The altar is anointed with Chrism, perfumed oil that is consecrated by the bishop during Holy Week each year. The anointing makes the altar a symbol of Christ, who before all others is called "The Anointed One". It is this reason the presider bows to and kisses the altar at the beginning and the end of Mass, and that those in the assembly show proper reverence by bowing to it. By anointing the altar, we set it aside solely for the purpose of celebrating the Eucharist.
>
> **Incensation of the Altar** – Incense is burned on the altar to signify that Christ's sacrifice there, perpetuated in mystery and ascends to God as an odor of sweetness. The incensation also signifies that the people's prayers rise up, pleasing and acceptable, piercing the clouds, reaching the throne of God.
>
> **Lighting of the Altar** – The lighting of the altar reminds us that Christ is the "light to enlighten the nations" (Luke 2:32); His brightness shines out in the Church and through it in the whole human family.
>
> **Covering of the Altar** – The covering of the altar indicates that the Christian altar of the Eucharistic sacrifice and the table of the Lord, around it priests and

I Am Proud to Be a Catholic!

people, by one and the same rite but with difference of function, celebrate the memorial of Christ's death and resurrection and partake of his supper. The altar is prepared as the table for the sacrificial banquet and adorned as for a feast. Thus the dressing of the altar clearly signifies that it is the Lord's table at which all God's people joyously meet to be refreshed with divine food, namely, the body and blood of Christ sacrificed.

Beautiful, beautiful, beautiful!

+ + + + + + + + + +

Personal opportunities / challenges –

+   *Before, during and after Mass take notice of the reverence or lack of reverence that church attendees show to the altar. Many bow out of habit and show no reverence. Become one of those that very slowly and reverently bow to the altar. Set an example for those around you. Demonstrate that you recognize the holiness of the altar table. If the tabernacle holding the Body of Christ is located in the church, the tabernacle takes precedence over the altar and requires a genuflection.*

Seven Sacraments

Most of us memorized the definition of a Sacrament from the old Baltimore Catechism –

The Sacrament is an outward sign instituted by Christ to give grace.

The definition of a sacrament as defined by The Catechism of the Catholic Church, Second Edition, is similar but has been slightly expanded –

A Sacrament is an efficacious sign of grace, instituted by Christ and entrusted to the Church, by which divine life is dispensed to us through the work of the Holy Spirit. (CCC 774, 1131)

Life is both a physical and a spiritual journey. Just as we need nourishment for our bodies on a daily basis, the seven sacraments provide a follower of Christ with nourishment for the soul. Every sacrament received is a personal encounter with God the Father, Son and Holy Spirit; it is a touch point between earth and eternity.

The seven sacraments of the Catholic Church were given and sanctified by Jesus Christ, himself, as documented in the four gospels by Matthew, Mark, Luke and John.

The Church has categorized the seven Sacraments into the Sacraments of Initiation, Healing and Service.

- <u>Sacraments of Initiation</u> gives all Christians a foundation for a life within the Catholic Church. We are given new life in the sacrament of Baptism; we are strengthened by the sacrament

I Am Proud to Be a Catholic!

of Confirmation; we receive weekly/daily nourishment for our spiritual souls in the sacrament of the Eucharist.

- Baptism – sanctified with the baptism of Jesus Christ by John the Baptist in the river Jordan.
- Confirmation – the Holy Spirit's descent on the twelve apostles in the upper chamber represented by the tongues of fire as promised by Jesus Christ before His ascension back into heaven.
- Eucharist – bread and wine consecrated by Jesus Christ to His Body and Blood, the night before he died, given to the twelve apostles as a gift at the Last Supper with a command to "Do this in remembrance of me".

• Sacraments of Healing provides all people with the gift of spiritual and physical healing as practiced by Jesus Christ throughout his three years of public life. The sacraments are an ongoing reconciliation of a sinful people to their Creator.

- Reconciliation – power granted to the eleven apostles by Jesus Christ shortly after His resurrection where He instructed them to forgive sin in the name of the Holy Spirit.
- Anointing of the sick – exampled by Jesus Christ as He healed the sick, raised the dead and forgave sin instructing his disciples to do the same – to cure the afflicted by casting out demons and anointing the sick with oil.

• Sacraments of Service are intended to endow those individuals with grace choosing a vocation in the service to others - to another individual in matrimony or to the members of the church of Christ as a Catholic priest. Both sacraments serve to sanctify the commitments made by an individual to someone else other than himself.

- Holy Orders – established by Jesus at the Last Supper in the selection of the twelve apostles to carry forth the work of His church. Catholic bishops, priests and deacons fulfill the responsibilities of apostolic succession.
- Matrimony – blessed and made a sacrament by Jesus Christ at the wedding feast of Cana.

Only the Catholic Church holds claim to the seven sacraments.

A bishop has the authority to gift all seven sacraments reserving exclusively to himself the sacraments of Holy Orders and Confirmation; the latter may be delegated to a priest.

A priest may gift the rites of Baptism, Eucharist, Reconciliation, Anointing of the Sick and witness the sacrament of Matrimony.

A deacon may gift the sacrament of Baptism and witness the sacrament of Matrimony.

+ + + + + + + + + +

Personal opportunities / challenges -

+ *Attend an Easter Vigil service and witness the three Sacraments of Initiation - Baptism, Confirmation and the Eucharist - received by an RCIA (Rites of Christian Initiation of Adults) candidate.*
+ *Read the Catechism of the Catholic Church (CCC) paragraphs 1210 through 1666, to develop a deeper understanding of each of the seven Sacraments. The Catechism goes into great detail discussing the graces of each of the Sacraments.*

Sacrament of Reconciliation

God loves us unconditionally! God loves us with such great intensity that He made us in His own image. As an extension of His love, He gave us a free will so we could freely love Him in return. Being human, God knew that we would fail and we would need His forgiveness.

After His resurrection Jesus gave us the sacrament of reconciliation -

> *"Then the disciples rejoiced when they saw the Lord. Jesus said to them again, "Peace be with you. As the Father has sent me, so I send you." When he had said this, he breathed on them and said to them, "Receive the Holy Spirit. If you forgive the sins of any, they are forgiven them; if you retain the sins of any, they are retained." (*John 20: 20a-23, NRSV)

Reconciliation is a gift from God. Just as the priest represents Jesus at the consecration of the Mass, the priest represents our heavenly Father during the sacrament of Reconciliation.

> *In the same way, I tell you, there will be more joy in heaven over one sinner who repents than over ninety-nine respectable people who do not need to repent."* (Luke 15: 7, NRSV)

The Sacrament of Reconciliation consists of

- Contrition – a true sorrow for one's sins with a firm intention to avoid further sin and a promise to do penance. The "Act of Contrition" is a confirmation of our intent.

Duane Crosland

> *"My God, I am sorry for my sins with all my heart. In choosing to do wrong and failing to do good, I have sinned against you whom I should love above all things. I firmly intend, with your help, to do penance, to sin no more, and to avoid whatever leads me to sin. Our Savior Jesus Christ suffered and died for us. In His name, my God, have mercy."*

- Confession – telling the kind and number of our sins to the priest; responding to any concerns the priest might have; listening to the words of advice from the priest.
- Penance – a prayer or an action requested by the priest to indicate a conversion of heart toward God and away from sin by the penitent.
- Absolution – the priest absolves the penitent of their sins "in the name of the Father, and of the Son, and of the Holy Spirit."

Homily of Pope John Paul II, September 13, 1987 –

> *"To those who have been far away from the sacrament of Reconciliation and forgiving love I make this appeal: come back to this source of grace; do not be afraid! Christ Himself is waiting for you. He will heal you, and you will be at peace with God."*

+ + + + + + + + + +

Personal opportunities / challenges –

+ *If you not been to the Sacrament of Reconciliation for a "long time", this opportunity / challenge, of course, will make you very nervous and anxious. Here is the opportunity / challenge I give to you - get to the Sacrament as soon as possible. God is waiting for you. I tell my fourth grade students that the priest will never raise his voice. God has made all priests "fishers of men." After the*

I Am Proud to Be a Catholic!

blessing and absolution, Jesus and the priest will both be happy. Jesus, the Good Shepard, will be happy because one of His sheep has returned to the fold. The priest will be happy because he has caught another fish for God!

+ *Enjoy the peace that will come from a good confession. Treat yourself to an ice cream cone or another refreshment of your choice. Peace!*

+ *How often a person should receive the Sacrament of Reconciliation varies by source; monthly is often mentioned. Find a schedule that you are comfortable with. One confession is better than no confessions! Each time you go you have a personal encounter with God the Father, Son and Holy Spirit.*

+ *Reminder – serious sin always requires the Sacrament of Reconciliation.*

Sign of the Cross

Most of us make the sign of the cross without contemplating its true significance. We bless ourselves as a matter of routine -

In the name of the Father
and of the Son
and of the Holy Spirit. Amen.

Each time we bless ourselves, we are professing our belief in the one true God, the Mystery of the Holy Trinity - God the Father, God the Son and God the Holy Spirit.

We are professing our belief in a God that <u>always was, is now</u> and <u>will always be</u>. The Sign of the Cross is our witness to the world that we are a Catholic.

The Sign of the Cross is unique to being a Catholic.

The Sign of the Cross is an integral part of the Sacrament of Baptism which initiates us into the Catholic Church; the sacrament that makes us children of God –

I baptize you in the name of the Father
and of the Son
and of the Holy Spirit.

The sign of the cross confirms that we belong to Christ. A prayer so simple is yet so profound!

+ + + + + + + + + +

Personal opportunities / challenges -

+ *Make a statement! When eating out at a restaurant, before eating your meal, make the Sign of the Cross followed by a prayer thanking God for His generosity. You will surprise God and you will most likely impress another patron in the restaurant for living your Catholic beliefs.*
+ *If you are a parent or grandparent make the sign of the cross on the forehead of your child/grandchild as you are kissing them goodbye or kissing them good night. Let them know that they are loved by God. Build a unique bond with your child/grandchildren using the Sign of the Cross.*

Catechism of the Catholic Church

The "Catechism of the Catholic Church" is a detailed summary of Catholic teachings; it is a teaching tool. The current version was commissioned by Pope John Paul II in support of the Vatican II Council. The Catechism was the collaborative effort of twelve Cardinals and Bishops with "extensive consultation among all Catholic Bishops, their Episcopal Conferences or Synods, and of theological and catechetical institutes".

The Catechism has four parts –

- Part One: <u>The Profession of Faith</u> uses the Apostles' Creed as the structure to define our beliefs as Catholics.
- Part Two: <u>The Celebration of the Christian Mystery</u> centers us on the liturgy of the church and the seven sacraments.
- Part Three: <u>Life in Christ</u> focuses on the Beatitudes, morality, sin, virtues, social justice, the Mother Church and finishes with the Ten Commandments.
- Part Four: <u>Christian Prayer</u> discusses prayer and uses The Lord's Prayer to complete the beliefs of the Catholic Church.

The Catechism provides a consistent message for all Catholics across the world whether they are young or old, male or female, regardless of social standing or ethnic background. The Catechism is a collective summary of two thousand years of church learnings based on tradition, the Old and New Testaments, Doctors of the Church writings and church councils always under the guidance of the Holy Spirit.

It can be found in both hardback and paperback form and a copy of it should be found in the home of all practicing Catholics. A second book called "The Companion to the Catechism of the Catholic

Church" along with a bible provides supporting documentation to the Catechism.

Many of us old timers remember the old Baltimore Catechism consisting of 499 short questions and answers –"Why did God make us" with an answer of "God made us to show forth His goodness and to share with us His everlasting happiness in heaven."

The Catechism of the Catholic Church (CCC), Second Edition is a brilliantly written document, often poetic in nature, of God's plan for the salvation of mankind. It is a story. The first paragraph of the Catechism sets the stage –

> **God, infinitely perfect and blessed in himself, in a plan of sheer goodness freely created man to make him share in his own blessed life. For this reason, at every time and in every place, God draws close to man. He calls man to seek him, to know him, to love him with all his strength. He calls together all men, scattered and divided by sin, into the unit of his family, the Church. To accomplish this when the fullness of time had come, God sent his Son as Redeemer and Savior. In his Son and through him, he invites men to become, in the Holy Spirit, his adopted children and thus heirs of his blessed life.** (CCC 1)

People say that the social teachings of the Catholic Church are the best kept secrets of the Church. I maintain that the "Catechism of the Catholic Church" is the best kept secret.

Duane Crosland

++++++++++

Personal opportunities / challenges –

+ *Beg, borrow or purchase a copy of the Catechism of the Catholic Church (CCC). You can find clean used copies on the internet at a significantly reduced price or you can find an online version on the United States Conference of Catholic Bishops (USCCB) web site at <u>www.usccb.org</u>. At first glance the book can be overwhelming. It is two inches thick with small print. Start slow and then build.*
+ *In some archdioceses you may be able to find a class that will walk you through the Catechism. Use the Catechism as an alternative to reading the bible. You might enjoy the differences between the pace and style of the bible and the Catechism. Use one source to support your learnings from the other source.*
+ *Again, beg, borrow or purchase a copy of The Companion to the Catechism of the Catholic Church. This book is more than two inches thick and the print is smaller than the CCC. The Companion expands on the footnotes and references documented in the Catechism. It complements and enriches the reading of the Catechism.*

God's Covenants with Man

God has demonstrated his love for us by giving us covenants to live by – those found in the Old Testament and the one found in the New Testament.

The Old Testament includes covenants with Adam, Noah, Abraham and Moses. The primary covenant in the Old Testament is the agreement with Moses where God gave us the Ten Commandments written on two tablets of stone after He freed the Jewish people from the bonds of Egyptian slavery. The Ten Commandments are still relevant today and were etched within our hearts when we were born. If the Ten Commandments were faithfully followed, there would be no wars, no false idols, no terrorists, no killing, no thefts, no lying, no hunger, no corporate greed, no immoral behavior, no divorce, etc. The first three commandments tell us how to love and respect God. The last seven commandments tell us how to love and respect ourselves and our neighbors. We honor this covenant every time we remain faithful to the Ten Commandments –

1. I am the Lord your God, you shall not have strange gods before Me.
2. You shall not take the name of the Lord your God in vain.
3. Keep holy the Lord's Day.
4. Honor your father and mother.
5. You shall not kill.
6. You shall not commit adultery.
7. You shall not steal.
8. You shall not bear false against your neighbor.
9. You shall not covet your neighbor's wife.
10. You shall not cover your neighbor's goods.

The New Covenant, the death and resurrection of Jesus Christ, was foretold and given to us at the Last Supper when Jesus promised to be physically with us until the end of time. The new covenant is renewed with every celebration of the Eucharist.

> *Then he took a loaf of bread, and when he had given thanks, he broke it and gave it to them, "This is my body, which is given for you. Do this in remembrance of me." And he did the same with the cup after supper, saying, "This cup that is poured out for you is the <u>new covenant</u> in my blood."*
> (Luke 22: 19- 20, NRSV)

This covenant of the Eucharist complements and is the fulfillment of the Great Commandment of Love -

> *You shall love the Lord your God with all your heart, and with all your soul, and with all your mind. This is the greatest and the most first commandment. And a second is like it: You shall love your neighbor as yourself. On these two commandments hang all the law and prophets. (*Matthew 22: 37- 40, NRSV)

+ + + + + + + + +

Personal opportunities / challenges -

+ *Memorize the Ten Commandments given to Moses by God. You most likely learned them when a child; it is time to give yourself a refresher course. The Ten Commandments can be found in the Old Testament in the Book of Exodus, Chapter 20, and the Book of Deuteronomy, Chapter 5.*
+ *Find a copy of the movie "The Ten Commandments" staring Charles Heston and live the book of Exodus in living color.*

I Am Proud to Be a Catholic!

Witness God's interaction with sinful man. The movie is usually shown by one of the major television networks at Easter.
+ *Memorize the Two Great Commandments given to us by Jesus Christ as listed above.*
+ *Shortly before His death Jesus simplified His command to love one another. Look up John 13:34-35.*
+ *Receive the Eucharist often. This is our confirmation of God's covenant with man until the end of time.*

Precepts of the Church

The pope and bishops have established five precepts (CCC 2042) to support the teachings of the Church. They are -

1. You shall attend Mass on Sundays and holy days of obligation and rest from servile labor.
2. You shall confess your sins at least once a year.
3. You shall receive the sacrament of the Eucharist at least during the Easter season.
4. You shall observe the days of fasting and abstinence established by the Church.
5. You shall help to provide for the needs of the Church.

The Church, in its infinite wisdom, provides us with the five Precepts – all of which encourages a closer relationship with God.

The first and most important Precept clarifies the third Commandment to "Keep holy the Lord's Day." Weekly attendance at Mass on Sundays is a requirement to being a Catholic. The second and third Precepts invite us to grow closer to the risen Lord through the Sacraments of Penance and the Eucharist. The fourth Precept helps us to redirect our attention from earthly distractions back to our God. The last Precept supports the growth of local and missionary efforts of the church.

The precepts teach us how to act as members of the Church and to make sure that the Church has what it needs to serve its members and to grow both locally and across the world.

I Am Proud to Be a Catholic!

++++++++++

Personal opportunities / challenges -

+ *All fraternities, clubs, organizations, business have rules / guidelines for their members. The Catholic Church is no different in this perspective. The bishops, in union with the Pope, have established the five precepts.*
+ *Given our societal mentality, the first precept is most likely the hardest to follow. Sunday has become another day during which we start and/or finish our weekly tasks.* **Sunday must clearly be defined as God's day.** *I teach my 4th grade students that to fulfill this precept and the Third Commandment they must -*

  – attend Sunday Mass
  – abstain from unnecessary work
  – enjoy time with family and friends.

  God rested on the seventh day setting Himself as an example to His creation. Very directly God tells us to "Keep My Day Holy".

+ *Reminder – for the dioceses of the United States the days for fasting are Ash Wednesday and Good Friday. The days of abstinence are Ash Wednesday and all Fridays during Lent.*

Perpetual Adoration

Jesus Christ, the Bread of Life, the Blessed Sacrament, the Holy Eucharist is made visible within a parish chapel in a monstrance for Perpetual Adoration.

A church having a large membership, Perpetual Adoration may be scheduled every day around the clock; parishioners are scheduled to be in the chapel hourly throughout the day and night. Some hours may have multiple worshipers. Some parishioners may not have an assigned time but will simply stop in for a visit with the Lord. Smaller churches may have a limited schedule throughout the week.

A chapel of Perpetual Adoration is a source of an amazing abundance of grace for the people of a church and the community.

Perpetual Adoration is a time for thoughtful prayer, spiritual reading, meditation, contemplation; a time to cry, to praise, to give glory, to petition; a time quietly listening for what Jesus might want to share with you; or a time simply gazing at our Lord while He gazes at you!

> *For we observed his star at its rising and have come to pay him homage.* (Matthew 2: 2a, NRSV)

Those who participate in Perpetual Adoration follow in the footsteps of the three kings as they searched for the infant Jesus. Coming from the East, the magi followed the star to the stable in Bethlehem to pay homage to the King. Two thousand years later we, too, "observe his star" and come to pay homage to the King.

I Am Proud to Be a Catholic!

+ + + + + + + + + +

Personal opportunities / challenges -

+ *Read the story of the magi as they journeyed from the East to find their King (Matthew 2:1-12). Put yourself in the story. Hold the gold in your hands, smell the frankincense, feel the myrrh as you enter a humble stable filled with animals. Behold, we have found the Messiah? Yes, we have!*
+ *Find a church with a Perpetual Adoration chapel and make the journey to find your King. When you find the Child in the manger, how will you act, what gifts will you bring, what will He want to tell you?*
+ *If your church has a Perpetual Adoration chapel, schedule a time for a weekly visit. If you have a tough schedule initially, try it for the Season of Advent or the Season of Lent. Your rewards will be great!*
+ *If not for an hour, how about 10 minutes? When our deacon comes to work in the morning, he always stops at the chapel for just a couple of minutes.*
+ *When in the chapel simply stop doing everything! Take time to gaze at Jesus Christ and let Him gaze at you. Live, feel, celebrate the Divine Presence!*
+ *Perpetual adoration is prep time for your time with God for eternity.*
+ *Growing up, I learned from my mother a very simple verse -*

Every time I pass a church,
I always stop in.
So, when I am carried in,
the Lord won't say – who is it?

Catholic Social Teaching

In 1995, the United States Conference of Catholic Bishops met to produce a summary of Catholic social teachings to be used as tool and a source for schools and parishes throughout the United States. The summary, *Sharing Catholic Social Teaching: Challenges and Directions,* is to be used as a starting point for those interested in pursuing Catholic social teachings in more detail. The seven themes are –

1. Life and dignity of the human person
2. Call to family, community and participation
3. Rights and responsibilities
4. Options for the poor and vulnerable
5. The dignity of work and rights of workers
6. Solidarity
7. Care of God's creation.

The full document can be found on the website of the United States Conference of Catholic Bishops www.usccb.org.

Throughout the document the Church's emphasis is on addressing poverty by enabling the poor to advance through productivity and earning fair pay while respecting the dignity of the individual and human life from conception to natural death.

On a personal note: my parish offered a 30 week course called "JustFaith" that walked a participant through various social issues of our time. Some of the topics covered were racism, hunger, life in third world countries, life in Harlem, immigration, use and sharing of world resources and social justice leaders of our time.

"JustFaith" touches on the seven points listed above and can prove to be a highly emotional roller coaster experience as you become a witness to the hardships that God's children are asked to endure.

I Am Proud to Be a Catholic!

- To witness life spent in a trash pile in the Philippines – from birth to death is beyond our imagination.
- To witness the life of an immigrant attempting to cross a desert to find a better life for his family, with a couple gallons of water and no earthly possessions, only to face death a few miles from a better life is again beyond our imagination.
- To read about some of the prominent social justice leaders past (Martin Luther King, Dorothy Day, etc) and present and their accomplishments are truly an inspiration.

Extensive reading is required and course sponsored visits to the inner city are encouraged.

"JustFaith" is a national initiative and can be found throughout the United States. Abbreviated versions and a version for teenagers are also available.

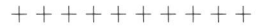

+ + + + + + + + + +

Personal opportunities / challenges -

+ Participate in a JustFaith discussion group. JustFaith Ministries, founded by Jack Jezreel, can be accessed at www.justfaith.org. Check with your archdiocese to see if the ministry is being offered locally. Since 1989 over 30,000 people have participated in various JustFaith programs in 1,500 churches across the country.
+ The book "The Challenge and Spirituality of Catholic Social Teaching", authored by Marvin L. Krier Mich, walks a reader through the seven Catholic social justice principles.
+ "Cloud of Witnesses" written by Jim Wallis and Joyce Hollyday, introduces a company of modern witnesses--saints, peacemakers, and martyrs who have embodied the gospel challenge of our time - Dietrich Bonhoeffer, martyr to the Nazis; Thomas Merton, the Trappist monk and prophet of

peace; Dorothy Day, Saint Francis of Assisi and many others from around the world. The book tells the story of simple people who accepted the challenges to change the world that they lived in.

Stations of the Cross

The devotion consists of meditating on fourteen events which took place during Christ's passion and death, from being condemned by Pilot to His burial in the tomb. The Stations are a tradition of Catholicism. The number 14 was fixed in 1731 by Pope Clement XII.

The practice started when Christian pilgrims to the Holy Land would walk the route that Jesus took as He made His way to Golgotha. The walk was called the "Via Dolorosa" or the Way of the Tears. Franciscan priest and brothers, as custodians of the "Via Dolorosa", encouraged and promoted the devotion. The devotion was later replicated at sites throughout Europe for those who could not journey to Jerusalem. Today, the Stations of the Cross can be found along the outer walls of our Catholic churches. The fourteen Stations of the Cross are -

    I.   Jesus is Condemned to Die
    II.   Jesus is Made to Bear His Cross
    III. Jesus Falls the First Time
    IV. Jesus Meets His Mother
    V.   Simon Helps Jesus Carry His Cross
    VI. Veronica Wipes the Face of Jesus
    VII. Jesus Falls the Second Time
    VIII. Jesus Meets the Women of Jerusalem
    IX. Jesus Falls the Third Time
    X.   Jesus is Stripped of His Clothing
    XI. Jesus is Nailed to the Cross
    XII. Jesus Dies on the Cross
    XIII. Jesus is Taken Down from the Cross
    XIV. Jesus is Laid in the Tomb

The most common format of the devotion at each of the 14 stations begins with "We adore Thee, O Christ, and we praise Thee - because by Thy holy cross Thou hast redeemed the world." followed by a short meditation, prayer and successive stanzas of the hymn, *Stabat Mater*.

The devotion of the Stations of the Cross can be found in most Catholic Churches on Friday evenings during the season of Lent and then on Good Friday in the afternoon between noon and 3 P.M.. Many churches offer a Lenten meatless meal before the Stations of the Cross.

A priest, a deacon or a lay person may lead the congregation in the prayers. Various formats are available. Some churches encourage their high school students to present the Stations of the Cross as a shadow show, students replicating the primary participants of each station as statue figures or a student led live reenactment of each station.

The Stations of the Cross is always a somber celebration appropriate for the Season of Lent but encouraged to be practiced throughout the church year.

+ + + + + + + + + +

Personal opportunities / challenges -

+ Walk the Stations of the Cross. Older churches tend to have more detailed and beautiful stations. As you progress through the stations what role do you take in the crucifixion and death of Christ? Were you Pontius Pilate, Simon of Cyrene, a soldier that nailed Jesus hands to the cross, a woman of Jerusalem?
+ Find a local church that offers the Stations of the Cross during Lent and plan to go. They might even offer a Lenten dinner prior to the stations.

Mary, the Mother of God

Mary, the mother of God, is also our spiritual mother given to us as Jesus hung on the cross moments before he uttered "It is finished".

> *Standing close to Jesus' cross were His mother, His mother's sister, Mary the wife of Cleophas, and Mary Magdalene. Jesus saw His mother and the disciple He loved standing there; so He said to His mother, "He is your son." Then He said to the disciple, "She is your mother."* (John 19: 25-27a, NRSV)

These words established a special relationship between the mother of God and all followers of Christ. The apostle John was our representative at the foot of the cross.

Mary found favor with God at the moment of her conception being conceived without original sin to prepare a sacred womb to conceive and bear the Son of God, the Son of Man.

> *When Mary's cousin Elizabeth was told that Mary was with child, Elizabeth, filled with the Holy Spirit, cried out in a loud voice and said, "Most blessed are you among women, and blessed is the fruit of your womb."* (Luke 1:42, NRSV)

Being the Mother of God, Mary is considered to be the greatest of all saints. As Catholics, we worship and adore only God but we honor Mary through prayer asking for her intercession with her Son.

The Catholic Church has documented proof of Mary's appearance over the centuries, usually to children of humble origin – Lourdes, Fatima, Guadalupe, etc.

Shrines have been built across the world dedicated to the Mother of God. The largest in the United States is the Basilica of the National Shrine of the Immaculate Conception located in Washington DC. A local shrine is the Shrine of Our Lady of Guadalupe located in La Crosse, Wisconsin.

Titles given to Mary by the Catholic Church are too numerous to list but some of them are Patroness of the United States, Blessed Virgin Mary, Queen of the Universe, Mother of God, Mother of the Church, Our Lady of Guadalupe, etc.

Special holy days dedicated to the Blessed Virgin Mary include -

- January 1 – Solemnity of Mary, Mother of God. The day is observed as a Holy Day of Obligation in the United States.
- March 25 – The Annunciation when the Archangel, Gabriel, announced to Mary that she would bear a son and call him Jesus.
- May 31 – The Visitation of Mary to her cousin Elizabeth who was with child – St John the Baptist.
- August 15 – The Assumption celebrates Mary being assumed into Heaven. The day is observed as a Holy Day of Obligation in the United States.
- September 8 – The Birth of Mary nine months after her Immaculate Conception.
- December 8 – Immaculate Conception celebrates the conception of Mary in the womb of her mother, St. Anne, by St. Joachim. Mary was conceived without sin. The day is observed as a Holy Day of Obligation in the United States.
- December 12 – Our Lady of Guadalupe.

The following chapter is on the Rosary which is the primary prayer dedicated to Mary.

I Am Proud to Be a Catholic!

+ + + + + + + + + +

Personal opportunities / challenges -

+ Visit a Marian Shine. Locally, there is Our Lady of Guadalupe, La Crosse, Wisconsin. Web site can be accessed at www.guadalupeshrine.org.
+ When in Washington D.C. make a visit to the Basilica of the National Shrine of the Immaculate Conception. Web site can be accessed at www.nationalshrine.com.
+ Watch the movie "Mary of Nazareth" directed by Giacomo Campiotti. Movie is a beautiful story of the life of Jesus Christ as told by Mary, the Mother of God. Movie can be ordered at www.maryfilm.com.
+ Take the time to understand the words of the Hail Mary prayer; the first part of the prayer is totally biblically based. "Hail Mary, full of Grace. The Lord is with thee." are the words used by the Angel Gabriel at the Annunciation. "Blessed are you among women, and blessed is the fruit of your womb." are the words used by Mary's cousin, Elizabeth, at the Visitation. The last half of the pray is our plea to Mary to intercede on our behalf with her Son now and at the hour of our death.

Rosary

The Rosary is a beautiful tapestry telling a story of the life of Jesus Christ often seen through the eyes of His Mother, Mary. For many Catholics, the Rosary is second in prayer only to the mass as it retells the birth, life and death of our Lord, Jesus Christ.

The origination of the Rosary is in question. It is thought that it evolved between the 12th and 15th century. There is evidence that "prayer bead" concept was used by the early church and may have been actually used prior to Christianity. Some sources give credit to Saint Dominic (d.1221) but there is no documented evidence to support this thought.

The Rosary evolved over centuries to include the Joyful, Sorrowful and Glorious Mysteries. In 2002 Pope John Paul added the Luminous Mysteries to cover the public ministry of Jesus Christ – the time between His Baptism and His gift of the Eucharist. In his document on the Rosary, Pope John Paul II reminded us –

> **The Rosary, though clearly Marian in character, is at heart a Christ-centered prayer.**

In 1571 Pope Pius V asked all Christian to say the Rosary in anticipation of a battle against the Muslims which greatly outnumbered the Christian military force. On October 7, 1571 the Muslims were defeated at the Battle of Lepanto. In 1572 Pope Pius V established the Feast of the Holy Rosary in memory of and to give thanks to Jesus Christ and His Mother for the victory at Lepanto.

As Catholics, we pray the Rosary asking Mary, as the Mother of Jesus Christ, to intercede with her Son on our behalf. We, along with Mary, share in the communion of saints. Mary is venerated; Mary is not worshipped; God alone is worshipped.

I Am Proud to Be a Catholic!

The Mysteries of the Rosary are -

- **Joyful Mysteries** joyfully celebrate the events that surround Jesus' birth and childhood.

  - The Annunciation – the Angel Gabriel tells Mary that she is to be the Mother of God (Luke 1:26–27)
  - The Visitation – Mary's visit to Elizabeth, the mother to be of John the Baptist (Luke 1;39-42)
  - The Nativity - Jesus Christ, the Son of God is born in a Bethlehem stable (Luke 2:1-7)
  - The Presentation of Jesus in the Temple (Luke 2:21-24)
  - The Finding of Jesus in the Temple by Mary and Joseph (Luke 2:41-47)

- **Luminous Mysteries** bear witness to Jesus' public ministry including the gift of the Eucharist.

  - The Baptism of Jesus in the river Jordan (Matthew 3:16-17)
  - The Wedding Feast of Cana (John 2:1-5)
  - Jesus' Proclamation of the Kingdom of God (Mark 1:15)
  - The Transfiguration of Jesus before Peter, James and John (Matthew 17:1-2)
  - The Gift of the Eucharist at the Last Supper (Matthew 26:26)

- **Sorrowful Mysteries** mournfully walks us through the passion and death of Jesus, Our Savior.

  - The Agony of Jesus in the Garden (Matthew 26:36-39)
  - The Scourging of Jesus at the Pillar (John 19:1-3)
  - The Crowning of Jesus with Thorns (Matthew 27:27-29)
  - The Carrying of the Cross by Jesus (Mark 15:21-22)
  - The Crucifixion and Death of Jesus (Luke 23:33-46)

- **Glorious Mysteries** triumphantly recalls the victories of the Resurrection, the descent of the Holy Spirit and the coronation of Mary as the Mother of God.

    - The Resurrection of Jesus (Luke 24:1-5)
    - The Ascension of Jesus into Heaven (Mark 16:19)
    - The Descent of the Holy Spirit upon the Apostles (Acts 2:1-4)
    - The Assumption of the Blessed Virgin Mary into Heaven (Luke 1:48-49)
    - The Coronation of Mary, the Mother of God as the Queen of heaven and earth (Rev 12:1)

The Rosary consists of a series of prayers –

- Sign of the Cross
- Apostles Creed
- Our Father
- Hail Mary (3)
- Glory Be
- Fatima Prayer
- Five repetitions – selecting one of the four mysteries listed above

    - Our Father
    - Hail Mary (10)
    - Glory Be
    - Fatima Prayer

- Hail Holy Queen
- Sign of the Cross

See the appendix in the back of the book for -

- *Common Catholic Prayers* to find the details of the prayers listed above.
- *Fifteen Promises of Mary* to those who pray the Rosary.

I Am Proud to Be a Catholic!

Also, see *Common Catholic Prayers* in the appendix for additional prayers common to practicing the Catholic faith.

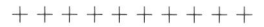

+ + + + + + + + +

Personal opportunities / challenges -

+ *Put the Rosary on the table. Go to your closet, storage area or book shelf to find a picture album of your family. Page through the picture album. Run your hands across the cover and think back to the activities that made this a story of your family. Then using the twenty decades of the Rosary let Mary walk you through her picture book from the Annunciation, through the birth, death and resurrection of her son and finally to her coronation in heaven. This is a story of Mary's family! She would love to share it with you.*
+ *Go to the Appendix and review the fifteen promises given to Saint Dominic and Blessed Alan by Our Lady for all those who faithfully pray the Rosary.*
+ *Find a scripture based Rosary guide. There is a short scripture reading for each Hail Mary to coincide with the decade being prayed. This may be a little more time consuming but it may keep you focused on the intent of the Rosary. Other variations to the scripture based Rosary can be purchased or found on the internet to aide in saying the prayer.*
+ *A number of my friends use a structured book called "Rosary Novenas to Our Lady" by ACTC publishing written by Charles V Lacey and updated by Gregory F. Augustine Pierce.*

Catholic Priest

The first Catholic priests were men called by Jesus to become His twelve apostles. Their names were Peter, Andrew, Matthew, Thomas, Philip, John, Jude, Bartholomew, James, Simon, James the Less and Judas Iscariot. Matthias was chosen as the 12th apostle after the death of Judas. Some were fishermen; one was a tax collector; others were followers of John the Baptist.

The twelve apostles were ordinary men called by Jesus to perform extraordinary acts of bravery in the name of their rabbi. They were men filled with a love and a passion for God. Except for John, eleven of the apostles were martyrs witnessing to the teachings of their leader and savior, Jesus Christ.

In roughly 90 AD Saint Ignatius of Antioch, student to Saint John, the Apostle, and third in line after Saint Peter, clearly defines the roles of deacon, priest (presbyter) and bishop in his letter to the Smyrnaeans, Chapter 9 -

> **Let all things therefore be done by you with good order in Christ. Let the laity be subject to the deacons; the deacons to the presbyters; the presbyters to the bishop; the bishop to Christ, even as He is to the Father.**

Today's bishops are the direct successors to the twelve apostles. As the Church grew, the privileges and responsibilities of the priesthood were shared with priests and deacons through the Sacrament of Ordination.

In the twenty-first century, Jesus continues to call men to the priesthood as successors to the twelve apostles. Pope Francis was an

I Am Proud to Be a Catholic!

ordinary man from Buenos Aires Argentina that responded to God's call to become a priest.

The Catholic priesthood is a participation in the priesthood of Christ and therefore traces its origin to Jesus Christ Himself when He chose the twelve apostles. To Peter, specifically, and the apostles, Jesus gave them keys to the kingdom of heaven.

As successors to the twelve apostles, bishops of today share the keys to the kingdom of heaven with priests specifically

- To change our gifts of bread and wine into the body and blood of Christ during the consecration of the Mass through the intercession of the Holy Spirit. Priests are the ordinary ministers of the Sacrament of the Eucharist.
- To forgive sins through the Sacrament of Reconciliation and the Sacrament of the Anointing of the Sick.

Priests and deacons are the ordinary ministers of the Sacrament of Baptism and witnesses to the Sacrament of Holy Matrimony.

Bishops are the ordinary ministers of the Sacrament of Holy Orders and the Sacrament of Confirmation although the latter may be shared with a priest.

Bishops, priests and deacons share the responsibility to spread the good news of the gospel.

Today's parish priest, although human and subject to personal failings is -

- the source of all sacramental graces given to us by Jesus Christ,
- the leader of biblical teachings as found in the Holy Bible,
- the teacher responsible for the fulfillment of Catholic traditions.

In summary I quote Saint John Chrysostrom -

> Priests have received a power which God has given neither to angels nor to archangels. It was said to them: 'Whatsoever you shall bind on earth shall be bound in heaven; and whatsoever you shall loose, shall be loosed.' Temporal rulers have indeed the power of binding; but they can only bind the body. Priests, in contrast, can bind with a bond which pertains to the soul itself and transcends the very heavens. Did [God] not give them all the powers of heaven? What greater power is there than this? The Father has given all judgment to the Son. And now I see the Son placing all this power in the hands of men. They are raised to this dignity as if they were already gathered up to heaven.

I Am Proud to Be a Catholic!

++++++++++

Personal opportunities / challenges -

+ *Befriend your local priest. Invite them out to lunch. Invite them to your home for a home cooked meal. For many it can be a lonely life going back to a rectory with the need to "make" a dinner.*
+ *Compliment a priest for the good work they do. Make sure your comments are 99.9% positive to balance the "constructive" comments that they receive on a daily basis.*
+ *At the end of the Sacrament of Reconciliation personally thank the priest for taking the time listening to your confession. Seasonally, wish them a Holy Child Filled Christmas or a Blessed Easter.*
+ *And most importantly, pray for our priests. They need your prayers to meet their daily challenges.*
+ *Our parish has a list of parishioners that have agreed to pray for our priests. If your parish does not have a prayer effort for your priest(s) start one with your friends.*

The Communion of Saints

The Communion of Saints beautifully defines the Body of Christ. This dogma of the faith can be found in the Apostles Creed –

I believe in the Holy Spirit, the holy Catholic Church, <u>the communion of saints</u>, the forgiveness of sins, the resurrection of the body, and life everlasting. Amen.

The Body of Christ includes His Church in heaven, on earth and those in purgatory waiting for their entrance into the heaven.

The Church <u>Triumphant</u> in heaven, the Church <u>Militant</u> on earth and the Church <u>Penitent</u> are united and all share in the life of Christ. These three entities form the communion of saints.

This belief is the basis that encourages us to pray to Mary, the Mother of God, and to the saints petitioning them to pray and to intercede for those on earth and for those in purgatory for the mercy of God.

+ + + + + + + + +

Personal opportunities / challenges -

+ *Per Oscar Wilde "Every saint has a past and every sinner has a future." This is the story of the communion of saints. Our lives on earth are intertwined with those in purgatory and those in heaven.*
+ *Reminder – we celebrate all the saints in heaven on November 1st of every year; the remembrance is called All Saints Day and is a Holy Day of Obligation.*
+ *We remember the souls in purgatory on November 2nd called All Souls Day; this day is not a Holy Day of Obligation.*

The Church Triumphant

The Church Triumphant is all the ordinary Catholic men and woman during the past two thousand years who accepted the invitation to follow in the footsteps of Jesus Christ; they fulfilled this invitation exceptionally well. These are the women and men who bravely and historically laid the basis for our current Catholic faith and continue to grow the Church. The Church Triumphant represents followers of Christ who are now in heaven confirmed either through miracles or personal acts of bravery.

Wikipedia https://en.wikipedia.org/wiki/List_of_saints lists 810 saints but readily admits that the numbers are more accurately in the thousands - many of them canonized before a documented process was established.

Catholics do not worship, adore nor praise the saints. Only God should be worshiped, adored and praised. In prayer Catholics ask the saints to intercede with God on their behalf for a specific request. Over time the Church has assigned saints to specific areas of need.

- St Peregrin is the patron saint for people with cancer.
- St Blaise is the patron saint for throat aliments.
- St Martha is the patron saint for waiters and waitresses.
- St Nicholas is the patron saint for Switzerland.
- St Luke is the patron saint for physicians.
- St Matthew is the patron saint for tax collectors.
- St Monica is the patron saint for mothers.
- Solemnity of the Immaculate Conception of Mary is the patron saint for the United States.

There is a saint assigned to almost every aspect of our lives which can be found on the internet.

Duane Crosland

To understand the scope of Church Triumphant I have categorized the saints into five major groupings.

Mary, Mother of God, is a saint but she is also the Mother of God's only Son, Jesus Christ. Thus, Mary, born without sin, is first among all the saints.

The **Apostles** were the twelve men personally chosen by Jesus Christ during His three years of public ministry. The twelve apostles are Peter (Simon), Andrew (brother to Simon Peter), James, (brother to James) John, Philip, Bartholomew, Thomas, Matthew, James, Thaddaeus, Simon and Matthias (chosen to replace Judas). With the exception of John, the Apostles all gave their lives as martyrs for their beliefs in the Catholic faith. These twelve men laid the seeds from which the Church grew. The twelve apostles are the source of Apostolic Succession – one of the four marks of the Catholic Church.

Doctor of the Church is a title given by the Catholic Church to individuals who contributed to the Church in the areas of prayer, doctrine, theology, or defended the Church against heresies. The Catholic Church has named 36 women and men as Doctors of the Church. A few of the better known ones are Teresa of Avila, Thomas Aquinas, Catherine of Siena, Augustine of Hippo, Theresa of Lisieux, Albertus Magnus and John of the Cross.

Martyrs are those that gave their life rather than deny the existence of Jesus Christ, His teachings and His Church. Martyrs recognized by the Church include –

- Saint Agnes – Agnes was born to Roman nobility in 291 A.D. and was beheaded at the age of 12 for her devotion and dedication to the Catholic faith.
- Saint Charles Lwanga and Companions – Charles was a Ugandan convert to Catholicism who along with twelve Catholic young

I Am Proud to Be a Catholic!

men and nine Anglicans were burned alive in 1886 when they refused to abandon their newly found faith.
- Saint Thomas More – Thomas, councilor to King Henry VIII, refused to pledge alliance to the King as Supreme Head of the Church of England. In 1535 Thomas was beheaded for treason.
- Saints Ignatius – Ignatius was a disciple of John the Apostle and the third bishop of Antioch. For his belief in Jesus Christ, he was fed to wild beasts in 108 A.D.
- Saint Isaac Jogues – Isaac was a Jesuit priest and missionary who worked among the American natives. In 1646 he was killed with a tomahawk by the Mohawk Indians and his body was thrown into the river.

The final group of saints I would like to mention are those men and woman who led **exemplary holy lives** and often served the poorest, most marginalized people in society throughout history. Some of the more easily recognizable saints are Saint Vincent de Paul, Saint John Paul II, Saint Margaret of Scotland, Saint Gemma Galgani, Saint Francis of Assisi, Saint Peter Claver, Saint Monica, Saint Joseph (husband to Mary), Saint Damien of Molokai, Saint John Vianney, Saint Monica, Saint Patrick and Saint Mary Magdalene; and the soon to be canonized saints are Louis and Marie Zelie Guerin Martin (parents of Saint Theresa of Lisieux) and Mother Teresa of Calcutta.

During our life time, Pope John Paul II canonized 110 saints, Pope Benedict canonized 41 saints and Pope Francis canonized 21 saints.

Duane Crosland

+ + + + + + + + + +

Personal opportunities / challenges -

+ *Details on individual saints can be found on the internet or in various books.*
+ *Carved stone statues and paintings of saints cover the old churches of Europe.*
+ *The modern churches found in the United States usually include a statue of Mary and Joseph and most likely a statue of the church's patron. My church, Saint Vincent de Paul Catholic Church, includes a statue of Saint Vincent de Paul in the gathering area of the church.*
+ *The Cathedral of Our Lady of the Angels located in Los Angeles, California, commissioned twenty-five tapestries picturing 135 saints and holy men and women that adorn the south and north walls of the Cathedral. A tapestry of St John the Baptist hangs over the baptistery. If in Los Angeles, a visit to the Cathedral is well worth your effort.*

The Beatitudes

The Beatitudes is the one teaching of Christ that is not unique to the Catholic Church. The Beatitudes are taught and shared by all Christian faiths. I made an exception to the Beatitudes for this book simply because they are simply too important not to include in the discussion of why "I Am Proud to be a Catholic."

Beatitudes

Blessed are the poor in spirit,
for theirs is the kingdom of heaven.
Blessed are those who mourn,
for they will be comforted.
Blessed are the meek,
for they will inherit the earth.
Blessed are those who hunger and thirst for
righteousness, for they will be filled.
Blessed are the merciful,
for they will receive mercy.
Blessed are the pure in heart,
for they will see God.
Blessed are the peacemakers,
for they will be called children of God.
Blessed are those who are persecuted for righteousness' sake,
for theirs is the kingdom of heaven.
(Matthew 5: 3-10, NRSV)

Jesus gave us the Beatitudes early in his ministry. Great crowds were following him on a daily basis as He traveled through Syria, Jordan, Judea, Jerusalem and Galilee. Jesus gifted us the Beatitudes on a small hill overlooking the Sea of Galilee; thus they are often referred to as the "Sermon on the Mount."

There are eight Beatitudes and they were given not "to abolish the law or the prophets" but "to fulfill" them.

The Greek translation for "blessed" is "happy". Thus, happy are those who attempt to follow the Beatitudes.

Simple and short explanations of the eight Beatitudes are -

- "poor in spirit" – we depend solely on God for all of our needs
- "who mourn" – we are saddened by the selfish behavior of others and try to make amends
- "are meek" – we are patient and respectful to others
- "hunger and thirst" – we search for justice for all people
- "merciful" – we forgive others and do not seek revenge
- "clean of heart" – we see God in all people and in all things
- "peacemakers" – we love and respect others and try to make true peace at all times
- "persecuted" – we are mistreated and judged because of our attempt to follow the teachings of Jesus Christ.

+ + + + + + + + +

Personal opportunities / challenges -

+ *The Beatitudes are meant to be memorized! This may take time and since they are conceptual in nature they may prove to be difficult to learn. The eight Beatitudes are Jesus' instructions to all of us as to how we are to live. They are meant to complement the Ten Commandments.*
+ *On a daily basis attempt to identify one action on your part where you are trying to live according to the Beatitudes. Be an example to those that you live with.*

Faith – A Belief in God

According to *The World Book Dictionary*, faith is 1) a believing without proof; trust; confidence, 2) belief in God or in God's promises, religion, or spiritual things.

An atheist has faith that the sun will rise tomorrow morning but an atheist does not believe in a god and specifically our God, the Holy Trinity.

Many people have faith that there is a God and in an afterlife but they take no action to grow their faith. Unfortunately, for many individuals faith diminishes as a person ages; they simply stop nurturing their faith at a time when they should be growing their faith in God.

Many of our Christian friends have a deep faith in God but their faith falls short of following the full range of teachings of Jesus Christ available only through the Catholic Church. Thus we have thousands of Christian churches each going in directions different from what Jesus Christ gave to us.

The eleven apostles lacked absolute faith as they huddled in the locked upper room. Jesus, their Savior, had been crucified and had risen from the dead when He left them to go back to the Father. The apostles were alone and afraid. The Holy Spirit had not yet come.

The virtue of Faith is necessary to being a Catholic; but the question must be asked – does God gift a person faith so that they might be a Catholic or does a person use the teachings, traditions and practices of the Catholic Church to grow their faith? Which comes first – the practice of Catholicism or the gift of Faith?

I personally see Faith as an intimate dance with God. A person needs to learn how to dance with God. Your first step on the dance floor may be a failure but God is there to encourage you on. Who takes the lead? Do you take the lead or do you let God take the lead? With each step you take, your faith in God has the potential to grow. Faith is dynamic and will grow daily if nurtured!

Per the Catechism of the Catholic Church, Faith is a supernatural gift and one of three theological virtues given to us by God at our Baptism; the other two virtues are Hope and Charity. God makes Faith available to all men but it is most often a person's freewill whether they grow or don't grow their faith. All people have faith but sometimes it is hidden and must be searched out and nurtured. Faith is the seed planted at Baptism within our souls and if properly nourished will give us eternal life.

I quote from the Catechism of the Catholic Church –

> **Faith is a personal adherence of the whole man to God who reveals himself. It involves an assent of the intellect and will to the self-revelation God has made through his deeds and words.** (CCC 176)

Pope John Paul II clearly and beautifully defines Faith similarly in a homily given in Brazil in 1991 -

> **Faith is a gift of God which reaches man through the message of absolute truth, but it is, at the same time, the response of the person who sincerely seeks an encounter with God.**

And finally from the Gospel of John, Jesus tells doubting Thomas -

> **Blessed are those who have not seen and have believed.** (John 20:29, NRSV)

On a personal note, do I have perfect faith? No! I have my moments of doubts; my moments of questioning; my moments of trying to rationalize something beyond my ability to reason. I sometimes examine other options but all my other options and conclusions have failed me. As Peter Simon responded to the Jesus Christ –

> **So Jesus asked the twelve, "Do you also wish to go away?" Simon Peter answered Him, "Lord, to whom can we go? You have the words of eternal life. We have come to believe and know that you are the Holy One of God."** (John 6:67-69, NRSV)

+ + + + + + + + + +

Personal opportunities / challenges -

+ *You have no faith in a God?*

- *The depth and breadth of the world we live in could only be created by a Being far superior to our capabilities and imagination.*
- *Step back and take a look at the world that surrounds you.*
- *On a clear night take a look at the setting sun, the rising moon, the stars and the planets that far exceed anything that our minds can grasp.*
- *Stop and feel your heart that has the capability to nurture your body without missing a beat for 100 years!*
- *Witness the unlimited variety of vegetation and animal life that exists across the world for our enjoyment and benefit.*
- *Look in a mirror and witness the inner soul given to you at your birth.*
- *Everything in the universe is in balance!*

+ *You have faith in God?*

- *Nurture it with daily prayer, reading the bible, attending weekly/daily mass, living a life according to the teachings and traditions of the Catholic Church.*

- Living a Christ-like life following the beatitudes and the Works of Mercy further enriches a person's faith life - always giving thanks to God for the gift of faith.

+ Whether you believe in God or don't believe in a god, I suggest you go to the internet and study Saint Thomas Aquinas' five Proofs of God's existence. You will find them interesting and thought provoking! One source is listed below-

    http://www.catholicforum.com/forums/showthread. php?3633-St-Thomas-Aquinas-5-proofs-of-God-s-existence.

    The five proofs that there is a living God according to Saint Thomas Aquinas are –

    - The Proof from Motion
    - The Proof from Efficient cause
    - The Proof from Necessary versus Possible Being
    - The Proof from Degrees of Perfection
    - The Proof from Design

Scandals of the Catholic Church

No, I am not proud of the scandals within the Catholic Church but I Am <u>still</u> Proud to be a Catholic. You may ask why I dedicate a chapter to this subject. Let me explain.

Recent scandals within the Catholic Church have dominated the headlines in news reports across the world of sexual abuse and the failure of our Church leaders to address these abuses. These and other scandals have been traced to the Vatican itself. We must bear witness to the Inquisition and the abuse of political power, positional influence and financial manipulation throughout our history. Unfortunately, there have always been and always will be scandals and human failings within the Catholic Church as a result of original sin.

Jesus Christ, the second person of the Trinity, is "alone holy" and the source of all that is pure and good. In choosing the twelve apostles, Jesus Christ knowingly called individuals with human frailties to be His followers.

Before Christ ascended into heaven, He clearly gave us examples that His Church would not be perfect.

- Peter denied Jesus three times but Peter clearly understood Jesus' teachings of forgiveness and mercy and was called by Jesus to be the first leader of His church.
- Judas sold Jesus for thirty pieces of silver but Judas did not understand Jesus' teachings of forgiveness and mercy.
- As Jesus hung on the cross, with the exception of His favorite disciple, John, and His mother, Mary, where were the other ten apostles?
- Thomas doubted the risen Christ until he was told to put his fingers into the wounds of Jesus.
- After the death of Jesus, the eleven apostles huddled in an upper room with locked doors in fear of the Jews.

If the *New York Times* existed in 33 A.D. the five failures on the part of the apostles would have made the headlines. These events would have been classified as scandals within a failed church.

The Church founded by Christ is firmly rooted in heaven but its leaders and members consist of men and women created by God with free wills. Free wills imply opportunities to fail balanced with opportunities for greatness, boldness and bravery.

Scandals are of men; scandals are not of the Church, nor of its founder, Jesus Christ.

Sources of scandal within the Catholic Church varied over the years and they are a part of who we are as humans and sinners.

In spite of scandals - the core teachings, traditions and beliefs of the Catholic Church remain rooted in Jesus Christ, our founder.

In Matthew Jesus instructs His followers –

> **therefore, do whatever they teach you and follow it; but do not do as they do for they do not practice what they teach.** (Matthew 23:3, NRSV)

On a very personal note, if you have forsaken the Catholic Church because of a known scandal or something that a priest said or did, I implore you to not let another person's behavior, another person's folly, affect your relationship with the church founded by Jesus Christ, the Son of God.

Per Father Peter Williams –

> **Keep your focus on the Eucharist and on Jesus Christ. All these scandal / distractions are the work of the devil.**

I Am Proud to Be a Catholic!

Forever remember that the Catholic Church is still the church given to us by Jesus Christ, Himself; it is a claim that no other church can make. The Catholic Church remains holy until the end of times no matter what scandals the devil gives to us.

I am and I will always be Proud to be a Catholic!

+ + + + + + + + + +

Personal opportunities / challenges -

+   *Learn the prayer to Saint Michael the Archangel to protect the church against the ruins of the devil –*

    "Saint Michael, the Archangel, defend us in battle. Be our protection against the wickedness and snares of the devil. May God rebuke him, we humbly pray; and do Thou, O Prince of the Heavenly Host, by the Divine Power of God, cast into hell Satan and all the evil spirits, who roam throughout the world seeking the ruin of souls. Amen."

+   *If you are a hesitant member of the Catholic Church because of the sins of one of its leaders, Jesus is waiting for your return. Just as Jesus forgave Peter, Jesus now extends His hand to you. Come back and rebuild a personal relationship with Jesus focused on the Eucharist.*
+   *Take advantage of various Child Protection programs and guidelines offered by dioceses throughout the United States.*
+   *In conversations about the Catholic Church be positive. Be aware of the efforts by The Dynamic Catholic Institute found at <u>www.dynamiccatholic.com</u>.*
+   *Read "Rediscover Catholicism" written by Matthew Kelly. The book is a spiritual guide to living with passion and purpose.*

The Catholic Church in the World Today

The Vatican estimates that there are 1.2 billion Catholics in the world today and 78 million Catholics in the United States.

Based on teachings from Jesus Christ –

> **Come, you that are blessed by my Father, inherit the kingdom prepared for you from the foundation of the world: for I was hungry and you gave me food, I was thirsty and you gave me something to drink, I was a stranger and you welcomed me, I was naked and you gave me clothing, I was sick and you took care of me, I was in prison and you visited me.** (Luke 25:34b-36, NRSV)

Catholics, throughout history, have been in the forefront of establishing schools, universities, orphanages, hospitals, food kitchens, shelters for the homeless, clothing distributions centers, day programs, refugee and immigration transitional services - locally and internationally. Within the United States, the Catholic Church, after the United States government, is second in providing assistance to those in need.

In addition to work performed and efforts supported at the parish level the United States Conference of Catholic Bishops (USCCB) formally established three initiatives to support the teachings of Jesus Christ -

- **Catholic Charities** to support local efforts
- **Campaign for Human Development** to address needs within the United States
- **Catholic Relief Services** to support international efforts.

Details for each of the organizations follow.

I Am Proud to Be a Catholic!

Catholic Charities (CC)

From the CC website www.catholiccharitiesusa.org -

The mission of Catholic Charities agencies is to provide service to people in need, to advocate for justice in social structures, and to call the entire church and other people of good will to do the same.

Catholic Charities is the largest private network of social service organization in the United States. It works to support families, reduce poverty, and build communities. Catholic Charities provides emergency and social services ranging from shelters and soup kitchens to day-care centers, summer camps, centers for seniors, and refugee resettlement offices for more than 10 million people. All major United States cities have locally managed Catholic Charities. The annual budget across all sites exceeds $2 billion.

Locally, Catholic Charities of Minneapolis / St Paul with a 2013 budget of $48 million provided assistance to 35,000 individuals and families, 467,000 nights to people in need of emergency shelters and one million meals. Six primary centers within the two cities are -

- Dorothy Day Center in St Paul and Higher Ground in Minneapolis (overnight and food distribution centers),
- St Joseph's Home for Children and Hope Street,
- Northside Child Development Center,
- Opportunity Center,
- Family Service Center.

All those in need are served regardless of creed, race or nationality.

Duane Crosland

Catholic Campaign for Human Development (CCHD)

From the CCHD website www.usccb.org –

The Catholic Campaign for Human Development (CCHD) was established by the United States Catholic Bishops in 1970 for the purpose of transforming lives and communities, focusing on breaking the cycle of poverty in thousands of communities across the United States with a twofold mandate: funding low-income controlled empowerment projects and educating Catholics about the root causes of poverty.

During the 2012-2013 grant period, the campaign gave out 214 grants in community and economic development, totaling more than $9 million.

CCHD brings the Gospel message to issues of social justice. The projects funded by CCHD focus on long-term solutions to poverty. This approach complements the work of direct-assistance programs like Catholic Charities.

Twenty-five percent of the proceeds from each CCHD collection stay in each diocese to fight poverty and foster liberty and justice at the local level. CCHD uses the national portion of the collection to fund projects across the country through grants. These grants fund community efforts to promote human dignity and fight poverty. Many of the funded projects focus on health care, immigration, community safety, political participation and environmental justice.

Being Catholic is not a consideration in making these grants, nor is this a means of converting people but of empowering people to work on a local level to make changes in their lives for the possibility of authentic human development.

I Am Proud to Be a Catholic!

Catholic Relief Services (CRS)

From the CRS website www.crs.org –

Catholic Relief Services (CRS), founded in 1943, is the official international humanitarian agency of the Catholic Community in the United States. In 2013 CRS provided assistance to 100 million people in 93 countries with an operating budget in the range of $600 million, without regard to race, religion or nationality.

Catholic Relief Services carries out the commitment of the Bishops of the United States to assist the poor and vulnerable overseas. CRS is motivated by the Gospel of Jesus Christ to cherish, preserve and uphold the sacredness and dignity of all human life, foster charity and justice, and embody Catholic social and moral teaching as we act to 1) promote human development by responding to major emergencies, fighting disease and poverty, and nurturing peaceful and just societies; 2) serve Catholics in the United States as they live their faith in solidarity with their brothers and sisters around the world.

As part of the universal mission of the Catholic Church, CRS works with local, national and international Catholic institutions and structures, as well as other organizations, to assist people on the basis of need, not creed, race or nationality.

Duane Crosland

+ + + + + + + + + +

Personal opportunities / challenges -

+ *Find a charity or an organization pursuing social justice issues that set your heart and soul on fire and then give to them generously – both financially and physically. No matter how little you have, someone in the world has less than what you have. Because of what you do today, someone in the world will live tomorrow.*
+ *Read Matthew 25:31-46. Jesus very clearly states that we will be judged on what we did to help our brothers and sisters. Learn the Works of Mercy –*

  – *Corporal Works for Mercy – Feed the hungry; give drink to the thirsty; cloth the naked; visit the imprisoned; shelter the homeless; visit the sick and bury the dead.*
  – *Spiritual Works of Mercy – Admonish the sinner; instruct the ignorant; counsel the doubtful; comfort the sorrowful; bear wrongs patiently; forgive all injuries and pray for the living and the dead.*

Closing Comments

On a Personal Note

After many years of asking myself why am I a Catholic, I can now comfortably say that I now know why I am a Catholic and why *"I Am Proud to be a Catholic."*

I am a Catholic for all the reasons found in this book. I love the founder, Jesus Christ. I love the rituals of the Mass and the 2000 years of tradition and biblical teachings. And most of all I love the Eucharist.

> **The Eucharist defines Catholicism and is unique to our Catholic faith. The Eucharist makes me proud to be a Catholic!**

I truly hope that this book helps you to confirm your beliefs in Jesus, your belief in His teachings, confirm your belief in His Church and most importantly confirm your belief in His gift of the Eucharist. Don't be the gentleman sitting in the front pew when the Bishop asks you "Why are you a Catholic?" and you have no good response.

If you are looking for a birthday or a Christmas gift for your child / grandchild that will pay endless rewards –

> **Tell your son, daughter, grandson and granddaughter why you are a Catholic. Tell them why you are proud to be a Catholic. This is important for them to hear over and over and over.**
>
> **Plant the seed! And then let God assume the responsibility to grow the faith.**

My parents planted the seed when I was very young and I clearly remember one moment in ninth grade when Brother Austin in room

213 at Cretin High School clearly stated in class that Christ gave us one Church and only one Church and it is the Catholic Church! Again, the seed had been planted and for me it took only 50 years for the seed to bear fruit.

In a couple of years, your children or grandchildren will be on their own and your influence as parents or grandparents will diminish. Ingrain these thoughts in them when they are receptive to new ideas. **Repeat them often!** Write them a letter to support your conversation. Put the letter in a safe place where they may refer to it at some later date. Give them a copy of this book with a short note written in the front of the book telling them why you are a Catholic. They may place your letter and the book on a shelf to be forgotten until some later date when you will have the chance to reinforce these beliefs.

Finally, I highly encourage you to attend Mass regularly with your family and specifically on Sundays and Holy Days of Obligation. This is our opportunity to come into physical contact with our GOD! Listen carefully to the words of the consecration – these are the same words that Jesus used at the Last Supper. Attending Mass gives you a front row seat to the Last Supper. The Last Supper / Sunday Mass should be the focus of a living relationship with our GOD. The bread and wine which become the body, blood, soul and divinity of Christ are the greatest gift anyone could give or receive. Keep your focus on the Eucharist!

I Am Proud to Be a Catholic!

+ + + + + + + + + +

Personal opportunities / challenges -

+ *If you are a Catholic, now it is your turn to say why you are Proud to be a Catholic! Be prepared for when the Bishop or a friend asks you – "Why are you a Catholic?"*
+ *If you are a Christian but not a practicing Catholic, I pray that I have enriched your faith journey. I would love to have a conversation with you.*
+ *At the end of this book I have included a page with perforated cards that state why I am Proud to be a Catholic. Take the page out of the book and keep a couple of cards in your purse or billfold. When the opportunity presents itself, pull out your card and share it with a friend.*

In closing –

I am Proud to be a Catholic! because ....

Duane S. Crosland, November 24, 2016

Appendix

Index of Religions & Date of Origination

- Judaism – at the direction of God, Abraham founded Judaism in the year 2000 B.C. in Canaan; today known as Israel.
- Hinduism – evolved 1,500 B.C. in India.
- Buddhism – Budda, Prince Siddhartha Gautama of India 563 B.C.
- **The Catholic Church – founded by Jesus Christ, 33 A.D.**
- Islam – Mohammed 600 A.D in Saudi Arabia.
- Eastern Orthodox sect separated from the Catholic Church in 1000 A.D. due to cultural difference.
- Lutheran – Martin Luther, Augustinian monk of the Catholic Church - 1517 A.D. initially in disagreement over the selling of indulgences. Excommunicated by the Catholic Church.
- Church of England / Anglican - established by King Henry the VIII in 1534 by law because Henry was not granted an annulment from Catherine of Aragon. Excommunicated by the Catholic Church.
- Methodist - founded by brothers John and Charles Wesley, Church of England / Anglican clergymen, in the early 1700's.
- Presbyterian - originally called Reformed, evolved from the mid 1500's to the mid 1600's led by John Knox based on John Calvin teachings.
- Unitarian – evolved from the 1500's through the early 1800's primarily in Hungary (Francis David), Poland (Faustus Socinus) and England (John Biddle).
- Congregationalist – branch of Puritanism 1600 England.
- Baptist – John Smyth, Church of England / Anglican clergyman, founded in Amsterdam 1607.
- Episcopalian – Samuel Seabury 1789 American colonies brought from England; is the United States version of the Anglican Church of England.
- Mormon (Latter Day Saints) – Joseph Smith founded in Palmyra, NY in 1830.

- Salvation Army – 1865 William Booth, a former Methodist preacher, in London.
- Christian Scientist – founded in 1879 by Mary Baker Eddy.
- Jehovah's Witness – founded in 1870 by Charles Taze Russell in Pennsylvania.
- Pentecostal – U. S. 1901.
- Agnostic – profess an uncertainty about the existence of a higher being.
- Atheist – do not believe in God or any higher being; Madelyn Murray O'Hair best known U.S. atheist.

In the United States of America it is estimated that there are 33,000 versions of Christianity and growing every day! In the Christian community only the Catholic Church can trace its founding back to Jesus Christ.

Fifteen Promises of Mary

In the thirteenth century, Saint Dominic and Blessed Alan received the following promises from Our Lady for all those who faithfully pray the Rosary:

1. Whosoever shall faithfully serve me by the recitation of the Rosary shall receive signal graces.
2. I promise my special protection and the greatest graces to all those who shall recite the Rosary.
3. The Rosary shall be a powerful armor against hell; it will destroy vice, decrease sin and defeat heresies.
4. It will cause good works to flourish; it will obtain for souls the abundant mercy of God; it will withdraw the hearts of men from the love of the world and its vanities, and will lift them to the desire for Eternal Things. Oh, those souls would sanctify themselves by this means.
5. The soul which recommends itself to me by the recitation of the Rosary shall not perish.
6. Whosoever shall recite the Rosary devoutly, applying himself to the consideration of its Sacred Mysteries shall never be conquered by misfortune. God will not chastise him in His justice, he shall not perish by an un-provided death; if he be just he shall remain in the grace of God, and become worthy of Eternal Life.
7. Whoever shall have a true devotion for the Rosary shall not die without the Sacraments of the Church.
8. Those who are faithful to recite the Rosary shall have during their life and at their death the Light of God and the plenitude of His Graces; at the moment of death they shall participate in the Merits of the Saints in Paradise.
9. I shall deliver from purgatory those who have been devoted to the Rosary.

10. The faithful children of the Rosary shall merit a high degree of Glory in Heaven.
11. You shall obtain all you ask of me by recitation of the Rosary.
12. All those who propagate the Holy Rosary shall be aided by me in their necessities.
13. I have obtained from my Divine Son that all the advocates of the Rosary shall have for intercessors the entire Celestial Court during their life and at the hour of death.
14. All who recite the Rosary are my Sons, and brothers of my Only Son Jesus Christ.
15. Devotion to my Rosary is a great sign of predestination.

Local and National Catholic Resources

St. George Catholic Books & Gifts
10904 Baltimore Street NE
Blaine, MN 55449
763-754-9777
www.stgeorgebooks.com

Leaflet Missal
976 West Minnehaha Avenue
St. Paul, MN 55104
651-487-2818
www.leafletonline.com

St. Patrick's Guild
1554 Randolph Avenue
St Paul, MN 55105
651-690-1506
www.stpatricksguild.com

Ignatius Press
1-888-615-3186
www.ignatius.com

Pauline Books and Media
617-522-8911
www.pauline.org

In His Name Catholic Store
919-847-2220
www.inhisname.com

Paulist Press
1-800-218-1903
www.paulistpress.com

Our Sunday Visitor
1-800-348-2440
www.osv.com

Loyola Press
1-800-621-1008
www.loyolapress.com

Common Catholic Prayers

Sign of the Cross

In the name of the Father and Son and Holy Spirit. Amen.

Apostles' Creed

I believe in God, the Father Almighty, Creator of heaven and earth; and in Jesus Christ, His only Son, our Lord: Who was conceived by the Holy Spirit, born of the Virgin Mary; suffered under Pontius Pilate, was crucified, died and was buried. He descended into hell; the third day He rose again from the dead; He ascended into heaven, is seated at the right hand of God the Father Almighty; from thence He shall come to judge the living and the dead. I believe in the Holy Spirit, the Holy Catholic Church, the communion of Saints, the forgiveness of sins, the resurrection of the body, and life everlasting. Amen.

Our Father

Our Father who art in heaven, hallowed be Thy name. Thy kingdom come. Thy will be done in earth, as it is in heaven. Give us this day our daily bread. And forgive us our trespasses, as we forgive those who trespass against us. And lead us not into temptation, but deliver us from evil. Amen. (Matthew 6:9-13)

Hail Mary

"Hail Mary full of Grace, the Lord is with thee." (Luke 1:28) "Blessed are thou among women and blessed is the fruit of thy womb Jesus." (Luke 1: 42b) Holy Mary Mother of God, pray for us sinners now and at the hour of our death Amen.

Glory be to the Father

Glory be to the Father, and to the Son, and to the Holy Spirit: As it was in the beginning, is now, and ever shall be, world without end. Amen.

Hail Holy Queen

Hail, holy Queen, Mother of mercy. Hail, our life, our sweetness and our hope. To thee do we cry, poor banished children of Eve. To thee do we send up our sighs, mourning and weeping in this vale of tears. Turn, then, most gracious Advocate, your eyes of mercy toward us; and after this, our exile, show unto us the blessed fruit of thy womb, Jesus, O clement, O loving, O sweet Virgin Mary! Amen.

I Am Proud to Be a Catholic!

Fatima Prayer

O My Jesus, forgive us our sins, save us from the fires of Hell and lead all souls to Heaven, especially those who are in most need of Thy mercy.

St. Michael the Archangel

St. Michael the Archangel, defend us in battle. Be our defense against the wickedness and snares of the Devil. May God rebuke him, we humbly pray, and do thou, O Prince of the heavenly hosts, by the power of God, thrust into hell Satan, and all the evil spirits, who prowl about the world seeking the ruin of souls. Amen.

Memorare

Remember, O most gracious Virgin Mary, that never was it known that anyone who fled to thy protection, implored thy help, or sought thine intercession was left unaided. Inspired by this confidence, I fly unto thee, O Virgin of virgins, my mother; to thee do I come, before thee I stand, sinful and sorrowful. O Mother of the Word Incarnate, despise not my petitions, but in thy mercy hear and answer me. Amen.

Grace Before Meals

Bless us, O Lord, and these Thy gifts, which we are about to receive from Thy bounty, through Christ our Lord. Amen.

Prayer of St John Vianney

I love You, O my God, and my only desire is to love You until the last breath of my life. I love You, O my infinitely lovable God, and I would rather die loving You, than live without loving You. I love You, Lord, and the only grace I ask is to love You eternally... My God, if my tongue cannot say in every moment that I love You, I want my heart to repeat it to You as often as I draw breath. (CCC 2658)

Prayer to the Holy Spirit

O, Holy Spirit, Beloved of my soul, I adore You. Enlighten me, guide me, strengthen me, console me. Tell me what I should do. Give me Your orders. I promise to submit myself to all that You desire of me and to accept all that You permit to happen to me. Let me know only Your will.

(Prayer by Cardinal Mercier found in "Be a Man!" Written by Father Larry Richard)

Act of Contrition

My God, I am sorry for my sins with all my heart. In choosing to do wrong and failing to do good, I have sinned against you whom I should love above all things. I firmly intend, with your help, to do penance, to sin no more, and to avoid whatever leads me to sin. Our Savior Jesus Christ suffered and died for us. In his name, my God, have mercy.

Duane Crosland

Holy God We Praise Thy Name

Holy God, we praise Thy Name; Lord of all, we bow before Thee! All on earth Thy scepter claim, All in heaven above adore Thee; Infinite Thy vast domain, Everlasting is Thy reign.

Hark the glad celestial hymn angel choirs above are raising; cherubim and seraphim, in unceasing chorus praising. Fill the heavens with sweet accord: Holy, holy, holy Lord.

Morning Offering Prayer

O Jesus, through the Immaculate Heart of Mary, I offer you my prayers, works, joys and sufferings of this day in union with the Holy Sacrifice of the Mass throughout the world. I offer them for all the intentions of your Sacred Heart: the salvation of souls, the reparation for sin, and the reunion of all Christians. I offer them for the intentions of our bishops and of all Apostles of Prayer, and in particular for those recommended by our Holy Father this month.

Chaplet of Divine Mercy

The Lord said to Blessed Faustina: "You will recite this chaplet on the beads of the Rosary in the following manner:"

Opening prayer say three times "O Blood and Water, which gushed forth from the Heart of Jesus as a font of mercy for us, I trust in You!"

Say one Our Father, one Hail Mary, and one Apostles' Creed.

On the Our Father Beads say "Eternal Father, I offer You the Body and Blood Soul and Divinity of Your dearly beloved Son, Our Lord Jesus Christ, in atonement for our sins and those of the whole world."

On the Hail Mary Beads say "For the sake of His sorrowful Passion, have mercy on us and on the whole world."

Concluding prayer say three times "Holy God, Holy Mighty One, Holy Immortal One, have mercy on us and on the whole world."

(Saint Maria Faustina Diary, 476)

I Am Proud to Be a Catholic!

Act of Faith *

O my God, I firmly believe that you are one God in three Divine Persons, Father, Son, and Holy Spirit; I believe that your Divine Son became man, and died for our sins, and that He will come to judge the living and the dead. I believe these and all the truths the Holy Catholic Church teaches because You have revealed them, who can neither deceive nor be deceived.

Act of Hope *

O my God, relying on Your almighty power and infinite mercy and promises, I hope to obtain pardon of my sins, the help of Your grace, and life everlasting, through the merits of Jesus Christ, my Lord and Redeemer.

Act of Love *

O my God, I love you above all things, with my whole heart and soul, because you are all-good and worthy of all love. I love my neighbor as myself for the love of you. I forgive all who have injured me, and I ask pardon of all whom I have injured.

* Variations may be found to the prayers listed above.

Tantum Ergo

Tantum ergo Sacramentum
Veneremur cernui:
Et antiquum documentum
Novo cedat ritui:
Praestet fides supplementum
Sensuum defectui.

Genitori, Genitoque
Laus et jubilatio,
Salus, honor, virtus quoque
Sit et benedictio:
Procedenti ab utroque
Compar sit laudatio. Amen.

Down in adoration falling,
Lo! the sacred Host we hail,
Lo! o'er ancient forms departing
Newer rites of grace prevail;
Faith for all defects supplying,
Where the feeble senses fail.

To the everlasting Father,
And the Son Who reigns on high
With the Holy Spirit proceeding
Forth from each eternally,
Be salvation, honor blessing,
Might and endless majesty. Amen.

(Written by Saint Thomas Aquinas in 1264 for the feast of Corpus Christi. Today sung at Benediction services.)

Litany's

Other beautiful prayers include -

- Litany of the Blessed Virgin Mary
- Litany of the Sacred Heart
- Litany of the Saints.

Notes

Notes

I AM PROUD TO BE A
Catholic!
- Jesus Christ, Founder / Foundation
- Sacrament of the Eucharist
- Sacrament of Reconciliation
- The Mass / Last Supper
- Perpetual Adoration
- Pope, Successor to St Peter
- Sign of the Cross
- Seven Sacraments
- Catholic Priest
- Mary, Mother of God
- Rosary

I AM PROUD TO BE A
Catholic!
- Jesus Christ, Founder / Foundation
- Sacrament of the Eucharist
- Sacrament of Reconciliation
- The Mass / Last Supper
- Perpetual Adoration
- Pope, Successor to St Peter
- Sign of the Cross
- Seven Sacraments
- Catholic Priest
- Mary, Mother of God
- Rosary

I AM PROUD TO BE A
Catholic!
- Jesus Christ, Founder / Foundation
- Sacrament of the Eucharist
- Sacrament of Reconciliation
- The Mass / Last Supper
- Perpetual Adoration
- Pope, Successor to St Peter
- Sign of the Cross
- Seven Sacraments
- Catholic Priest
- Mary, Mother of God
- Rosary

I AM PROUD TO BE A
Catholic!
- Jesus Christ, Founder / Foundation
- Sacrament of the Eucharist
- Sacrament of Reconciliation
- The Mass / Last Supper
- Perpetual Adoration
- Pope, Successor to St Peter
- Sign of the Cross
- Seven Sacraments
- Catholic Priest
- Mary, Mother of God
- Rosary

About the Author

Duane Crosland is active in his local church as a catechist, Eucharist minister, member of the Knights of Columbus Council 9139, Perpetual Adoration participant, a "40 Days for Life" organizer, and a parish coordinator for Feed My Starving Children, packing two million meals sent to God's starving children around the world. After thirty-five years with Ameriprise Financial, at the age of sixty-two, Duane realized that he was a "coasting" Catholic, unable to verbally answer the question as to why he was a practicing Catholic. He is a product of sixteen years of Catholic education—a graduate of the University of Saint Thomas, St. Paul, Minnesota, the Catechetical Institute, and JustFaith. Duane and his wife, Kay, live in Minnesota with their three sons and their families. Duane Crosland can be reached at dcrosl@aol.com.

Printed in the United States
By Bookmasters